A STORMY
SPANISH SUMMER

A STORMY
SPANISH SUMMER

BY

PENNY JORDAN

First published in Great Britain 2011
by Mills & Boon, an imprint of Harlequin (UK) Limited,
Large Print edition 2011
Eton House, 18-24 Paradise Road,
Richmond, Surrey TW9 1SR

© Penny Jordan 2011

ISBN: 978 0 263 22208 1

Harlequin (UK) policy is to use papers that are natural,
renewable and recyclable products and made from
wood grown in sustainable forests. The logging and
manufacturing process conform to the legal environmental
regulations of the country of origin.

Printed and bound in Great Britain
by CPI Antony Rowe, Chippenham, Wiltshire

CHAPTER ONE

'FELICITY.'

There was no emotion in the voice of the tall, dark-haired, aristocratic Spaniard looking down at her from his six-feet-plus height. No welcome of any kind for her. But even without the disapproval and the almost rigid distaste she could see in his expression, Felicity knew that Vidal y Salvadores, Duque de Fuentualba, would never welcome her presence here on his home soil— *her* home soil in one sense, given that her late father was Spanish.

Spanish, and Vidal's adopted uncle.

It had taken every bit of courage she'd had and nights of sleeplessness for her to come here, but there was no way she was going to let Vidal know that. No quarter would be asked from him by her, because she knew that none would be given. She had had proof of that.

Panic fluttered in her stomach, rising swiftly inside her to set her heart thudding and her pulse racing. She must not think about that. Not now, when she needed all her strength. When she knew that that strength would dissolve like a mirage in the heat of the Andalusian sun if she allowed those dreadful, shameful memories to surface and those sickening images to form inside her head.

Fliss felt she had never longed more for the comforting and supportive love of her mother— or even the courage-inducing presence of her trio of girlfriends. But they, like her mother, were now absent from her life. They might be alive, not dead like her mother, but their careers had taken them to distant parts of the world. Only she had remained in their home town, and was now its Deputy Tourism Director—a responsible, demanding job.

A job that meant she could tell herself she

was far too busy to have the time to build up a meaningful relationship with a man?

Thinking such thoughts was like biting down on a raw nerve in a tooth, the pain immediate and sharp. Better to think about why she had decided to use some of the leave entitlement she had built up through the long hours she worked in order to come here, when the reality was that her father's will could have been dealt with quite easily in her absence. That was certainly what Vidal would have wanted to happen.

Vidal.

If only she had the courage to fly free of her own past. If only she wasn't shackled to the past by a shame so bone deep that she could never escape from it. If only… There were so many if onlys in her life—most of them caused by Vidal.

In the heat of the concourse outside the busy Spanish airport into which she had just flown, filled with other people milling around them, he took a step towards her. Immediately she reacted, her body tensing in angry rejecting panic, her brain freezing so that she couldn't either speak or move.

It might have been seven years since she had last seen him, but she had recognised him immediately. Impossible for her not to do so when his features were cut so deep into her emotions. So deep and so poisonously that even now the wounds caused by those cuts had still not healed. That was nonsense, Fliss told herself. He had no power over her now—no power of any kind. And she was here to prove that to him.

'There was no need for you to meet me,' she told him, forcing herself to raise her head and look him in the eyes. Those eyes that had once looked at her in a way that had flayed the skin from her pride and her self-respect and left them raw and bleeding.

Her stomach churned again as she watched his far too handsome, arrogant, aristocratic male profile tighten into hauteur. His mouth curled in contemptuous disdain as he looked down at her, the late-afternoon Spanish sunlight shining on his thick dark hair. She was five feet seven, but she had to tilt her head back to meet his gaze, her own firing up from warm blue into heated violet as she met the look he was giving her.

She was hot and travel weary, and her body reacted to the unfamiliar heat as she resisted the need to lift the heavy weight of her thick, dark gold shoulder-length hair away from the back of her neck. She could already feel it starting to curl round her face in the humid heat, overcoming the effort she had made to straighten it into an immaculate elegance. Not that her appearance could ever compete with the true elegance of the smartly turned-out Spanish women around her. She favoured casual clothes, and was dressed in a pair of clean but well-washed and faded jeans, worn with a loose white cotton top. The jacket she had been wearing when she had boarded her flight in the UK was now stashed away in her roomy leather handbag.

Vidal frowned as his gaze was drawn

inexorably to the windblown sensuality of her naturally honey-streaked hair, reminding him of the last time he had seen it. Her hair, like her body, had been spread against her bed, enjoying the amorous attentions of the boy who had been fondling her before Vidal and her mother had interrupted their illicit intimacy.

Angrily Vidal looked away from her. Her presence here was unwanted and unwelcome, her morals an affront to everything he believed in, but like the dark matter at the heart of a poisoned wound there was also that kernel of self-knowledge that raked his pride and refused to be locked away and forgotten.

To have looked into the wanton sensuality of her face, to have witnessed the manner in which she, at sixteen already an experienced tramp, had flaunted that sensuality mockingly in front of him, without a trace of shame, should have filled him with disgust and nothing but disgust. Only along with that disgust, like a sword plunged straight through his body, there had been that momentary pride-searing, lightning surge of desire. It had burned a brand of searing self-contempt through him, and the embers had never fully cooled.

She might be able to get under his skin, but he could never allow her back into his heart.

She shouldn't have come here, Fliss told herself. Not knowing that she would have to confront Vidal. Not knowing what he thought about her and why. But how could she not have come? How could she have denied herself this final opportunity to know something of the man who had fathered her?

Unlike her, Vidal looked impeccably cool in the heat, his suit that shade of neutral light beige that only continental men seemed to be able to wear with confidence, the blue shirt he was wearing beneath his jacket somehow emphasising the falcon gold of his eyes. A hunter's eyes, a predator's eyes, cold with cruelty and menace. She knew she would never forget those eyes. They haunted her nightmares, their gaze sliding over her like ice, their chilling contempt burning her skin and her pride.

She was not going to allow Vidal to see how she felt, though. She wasn't going to shrink away in fear beneath their incisive, lacerating focus, just as she wasn't going to be intimidated by him. Only to herself was she prepared to admit that it had been a shock to find him waiting for her at the airport. She had not expected that—even though she had written to the lawyers informing them of her plans—plans she knew he would not like or approve of, but which she had no intention of changing. A thrill of triumph laced with adrenalin shot through her at the thought of getting the better of him.

'You haven't changed, Vidal,' she told him, summoning her courage. 'You still obviously hate the thought of me being my father's daughter. But then you would do, wouldn't you? After all, it was in part thanks to you that my parents were forced apart, wasn't it? You were the one who betrayed them to your grandmother.'

'They would never have been allowed to marry.'

Fliss knew that that was true—her mother had said so herself, with more sadness in her voice than bitterness—but Fliss wasn't going to give up the opportunity to seize the moral high ground from Vidal so easily.

'They might have found a way, if they'd had more time.'

Vidal looked away from her. Inside his head was a memory he didn't want to have brought back to him: the sound of his own seven-year-old voice, naively telling his grandmother about the way in which he and his au pair had unexpectedly bumped into his adopted uncle when she had taken him on a visit to the Alhambra—not realising then that his uncle was supposed to have been in Madrid on family business, and certainly not realising the significance of that seemingly unexpected meeting.

His grandmother had realised what it meant, though. Felipe had been the son of her oldest friend, Maria Romero, an impoverished but aristocratic widow. When Maria had learned she had terminal cancer, and only a matter of months to live, she'd asked her friend to adopt twelve-year-old Felipe after her death and raise him as her own son. Both his grandmother and Maria had held the old-school belief that those of certain families—of certain blood and tradition—should always and only marry those who shared those things.

Guilt. It was a heavy burden to bear.

'They would never have been allowed to marry,' he repeated.

He was hateful, arrogant, with a pride as cold as ice and as hard as granite, Fliss thought angrily. Technically her mother might have died from heart failure, but who was to say that part of that failure had not been caused by a broken heart and destroyed dreams? Her mother had only been thirty-seven when she'd died, and Fliss eighteen, just about to go to university. Eighteen and a girl still—but now, at twenty-three, she was a woman.

Was that a hint of guilty colour she could see burning up the golden skin bequeathed to him by generations of high-born nobles of supposedly pure Castilian blood? She doubted it. This man wasn't capable of such feelings—of any kind of real feelings for other people. His blood didn't allow that. Blood which some whispered had once been mixed with that of a Moorish princess coveted by the proud Castilian who was her family's enemy and who had stolen her away from that family for his own pleasure, giving to the wife who shared his bloodline the boy child born of his forbidden relationship, and leaving his stolen concubine to die of grief at the loss of her child.

Fliss could well imagine that a family that had spawned a man like the one standing in front of her now could have committed such a terrible act. When her mother had first told her the tale of that long-ago Castilian *duque* she had immediately linked him in her own thoughts to the current *duque*. They shared the same cruel disregard for the feelings of others, the same arrogant belief that who they were gave them the right to ride roughshod over other people, to make judgements about them and then condemn them without ever allowing them to defend themselves. The right to deny a child access to her father, prevent her knowing and loving her father simply because they did not consider that child 'good enough' to be a part of their family.

Her father. Inside her head Fliss tasted the words, rolling them round her tongue, their flavour and intimacy both confusing and new. She'd spent so much of her life secretly wondering about her father, secretly imagining them meeting, secretly wanting to bring about that meeting. At home, in her smart flat in an elegant Georgian house which had been converted into apartments set in beautifully maintained gardens, complete with a tennis court and an indoor swimming pool and gym for the use of the residents, Fliss had a box in which she kept all the letters she had secretly written to her father but never sent. Letters she had kept hidden from her mother, not wanting to hurt her. Letters that had never been sent—all bar one of them.

Her great-grandmother might have been the one to originally part her parents, but it was Vidal who had prevented *her* from making contact with him. Vidal who had denied her the right to get to know her father because he had not thought her 'good enough' to be acknowledged as part of his family.

At least her father had attempted to make some kind of reparation for allowing her to be shut out of his life.

'Why have you come here, Felicity?'

The coldness in Vidal's voice stirred Fliss's pride.

'You know perfectly well why I am here. I'm here because of my father's will.'

As she spoke the words *my father*, Fliss felt her emotions pushing up under the control she always tried to impose on them. There had been so much pain, so much confusion, so much shame within her over the years, born of the rejection of her and her mother by her father's family. And for her it was Vidal who personified that rejection. Vidal who'd denied and hurt her—in many ways far more than her father himself had.

Vidal. Fliss forced down the emotions threatening to swamp her, afraid of what might happen to her once they did, of what she might have to confront within herself once their roaring tide subsided, leaving her vulnerabilities revealed.

The truth was that she wasn't here because of any material benefit that accrued to her from her father's will, but because of the emotional benefit—the emotional healing she longed for so much. There was no power on this earth, though, that would ever be able to force her to reveal that truth to Vidal.

'There was no need for you to come here because of Felipe's will, Felicity. The letter his lawyer sent to you made the terms of it perfectly clear. Your presence here is neither needed nor necessary.'

'Just like in your eyes neither my mother nor I were needed in my father's life—not needed and not necessary. Quite the opposite, in fact. How arrogant you are, Vidal, to feel you have the right to make such judgements. But then you are very good at making judgements that affect the lives of others, aren't you? You think you are so much better than other people, but you aren't, Vidal. Despite your rank, despite the arrogance and pride you lay claim to through your Castilian blood, in reality you are less worthy of them than the poorest beggar in the streets of Granada. You despise others because you think you are superior to them, but the reality is that *you* are the one who should be treated with contempt. You are incapable of compassion or understanding. You are incapable of real emotions, Vidal, incapable of knowing what it truly means to be human,' Fliss told him emotionally, hurling the words at him as feelings she had suppressed for too long overwhelmed her.

White to the lips, Vidal listened to her. That she of all people should dare to make such accusations against him infuriated him.

'You know nothing of what I am,' he told her savagely.

'On the contrary—I know a great deal about you and what you are,' Fliss corrected him. 'You are the Duque de Fuentualba, a position you were born to fill—*created* to fill, in fact, since your parents' marriage was arranged by both their families in order to preserve the purity of their bloodline. You own vast tracts of land, both here and in South America, you represent and uphold a feudal system that requires others to submit to your power, and you think that gives you the right to treat them with contempt and disdain. It was because of *you* and what you are that I never got the chance to know my father whilst he was alive.'

'And now you are here to seek revenge? Is that what you are trying to tell me?'

'I don't need to seek revenge,' Fliss told him, fiercely repudiating his accusation. 'You will by your very nature bring that revenge down on your own head—although I am sure you won't even recognise it for what it is. Your nature, your outlook on life, will deny you exactly what you denied my parents—a happy, loving, committed lifelong relationship, entered into for no other reason than the two people within it loved one another. My revenge will be in knowing that you will never know what real happiness is— because you are not genetically capable of knowing it. You will never hold a woman's love, and most pitiful of all you will not even realise what you are missing.'

His very silence was unnerving on its own, without the look he was giving her, Fliss recognised. But she was not her gentle, vulnerable mother, made fearful and insignificant by a too arrogant man.

'Has no one ever told you that it can be dangerous to offer such opinions?'

'Maybe I don't care about inciting danger when it comes to speaking the truth,' Fliss answered, giving a small shrug as she added, 'After all, what more harm could you possibly do to me than the harm you have already done?'

That was as close as she dared allow herself to get to letting the pain inside her show. To say more would be too dangerous. She couldn't say any more without risking letting him see the scars he had inflicted so deep into everything that she was that she would bear them for ever. They—*he*—had changed her life for ever. Had deprived her of her right to love and be loved— not just as a daughter, but as a woman. But now was not the time to think of the damage that had been done to her, both to her emotions and her sensuality. She would never give Vidal the satisfaction of knowing just what he had done to her.

Vidal fought against the threat to his self-control. 'Let me assure you of one thing,' he announced grimly, each word carefully measured. 'When it comes to my marriage, the woman who becomes my wife will not be someone—'

'Like me?' Fliss supplied tauntingly for him.

'No man, if he is honest, wants as his wife someone whose sexual morals are those of the gutter. It is in the nature of the male to be protective of his chosen mate's virtue, to want the intimacy he shares with that mate to be exclusive. A man can never know for sure that any child his mate carries is truly his, therefore he instinctively seeks a mate whom he believes he can trust to be sexually loyal to him. When I marry my wife will know that she will have my commitment to her for our lifetime, and I will expect the same commitment from her.'

He was angry. Fliss could see that. But instead of intimidating her his anger exhilarated her. Exhilarated her and excited her, driving her to push him even harder, and to go on pushing him until she had pushed him beyond the boundary of his self-control. A frisson of unfamiliar emotion shivered down her spine. Vidal was a man of strong passions who kept those passions tightly leashed. The woman who could arouse them—and him—would have to be equally passionate, or risk being consumed in their fiery heat. In bed he would be…

Shocked, Fliss veered away from pursuing her own thoughts, her face starting to burn. What was happening to her? She felt as though she had been struck by a thunderbolt, the aftershock leaving her feeling sick and shaky. How could she have allowed herself to think like that about Vidal?

'You shouldn't have come here to Spain, Felicity.'

'You mean you didn't want me to come,' Fliss responded at Vidal's coldly delivered words. 'Well, I've got news for you, Vidal. I'm not sixteen any more, and you can't tell me what to do. Now, if you'll excuse me, I would like to go and check in to my hotel. There was no need for you to come here to the airport,' she told him, intent on dismissing him. 'We don't have anything to say to one another that can't be said tomorrow, at our meeting with my late father's attorney.'

She made to step past him, but as she did so his hand shot out, his long tanned fingers curling round her arm and restraining her. It seemed odd that such an elegant hand with such fastidiously well-cared-for nails could possess such feral male power, but it did, Fliss recognised as her flesh pulsed hotly beneath his hold. Her blood was beating with unfamiliar speed, as though responding to *his* command and not the command of her own body.

Her sharp, 'Let me go,' was met with a dark look.

'There is nothing I would like to do more, I assure you. But since my mother is expecting you to stay with us, and will be awaiting our arrival, I'm afraid that that is not possible.'

'Your mother?'

'Yes. She has come especially from her home

in the mountains to our townhouse, here in the city, so that she can welcome you into the family.'

'Welcome me into the family?' Fliss shot him a derisory look. 'Do you think I *want* that after the way "the family" treated my mother—the au pair not good enough to marry my father? The way they refused to acknowledge my existence?'

Ignoring Fliss's angry outburst as though she hadn't spoken, Vidal continued coldly, 'You should have thought of the consequences of coming here before you decided to do so—but then you are not someone who thinks it important to think of the consequences of your behaviour, are you, Felicity? Neither the consequences nor their effect on others.'

Fliss couldn't bring herself to look at him. Of course he *would* throw that at her. Of course he would.

'I have no wish to meet your mother. My hotel booking—'

'Has been cancelled.'

No, she couldn't. She wouldn't. Panic hit her. Fliss opened her mouth to protest, but it was too late. She was already being propelled firmly towards the car park. A sudden movement of the crowd pushed her closer to Vidal's side, and her own flesh was immediately aware of the male strength and heat of his body as her thigh came into brief contact with his, hard with muscle beneath the expensive fabric of his clothes. She recoiled, her mouth dry, her heart thudding, as memories she couldn't bear to relive mocked her attempts to deny them.

They moved swiftly along in the full glare and heat of the high summer sun—which was surely why her body had started to burn so hotly that she could feel the beat of her own blood in her face.

'You should be wearing a hat,' Vidal rebuked her, his critical gaze raking her hot face. 'You are too pale-skinned to be exposed to the full heat of our sun.'

It wasn't the sun that was the cause of the heat burning her, Fliss knew. But thankfully only she knew that.

'I have a hat in my case,' she told him. 'But since I expected to go straight to my hotel from the airport by taxi, rather than being virtually kidnapped and forced to stand in the sun's full glare, I didn't think it necessary.'

'The only reason you were standing anywhere was because you chose to create an argument. My car is over here,' Vidal told her. His arrogance caused Fliss to grit her teeth. How typical it was of everything she knew about him that he made no attempt to apologise and instead tried to put *her* in the wrong. He had lifted his hand, as though to place it against the small of her back and no doubt propel her in the direction of the waiting vehicle, but her immediate reaction was to step hurriedly away from him. She could not bear him to touch her. To do so would be a form of self-betrayal she could not endure. And besides, he was too… Too what? Too male?

He had seen her hasty movement, of course, and now he was looking at her in a way that locked her stomach muscles against the biting contempt of that look.

'It's too late for you to put on the "shrinking virgin, fearful of a man's touch" act for me,' he warned her

She wasn't going to let him speak to her like that. She couldn't.

'I'm not acting,' she told him. 'And it wasn't fear. It was revulsion.'

'You lost the right to that kind of chaste reaction a long time ago, and we both know it,' Vidal taunted.

Anger and something else—something aching and sad and lost—tightened painfully in her chest.

Once—also a long time ago, or so it seemed now—she had been a young girl trembling on the brink of her first emotional and sensual crush on a real-life adult man, seeing in him everything her romantic heart craved, and sensing in him the potential to fulfil every innocent sensual fantasy her emerging sexuality had had aching inside her. A sensation, lightning swift and electrifying, raced down her spine, sensitising her flesh and raising the tiny hairs at the nape of her neck.

A new shudder gripped her body. Fresh panic seized her. It must be the heat that was doing this to her. It couldn't be Vidal himself. It could not, *must* not be Vidal who was responsible for the sudden unnerving and wholly unwanted tremor of physical sensation that had traced a line of shockingly sensual fire down her spine. It was some kind of physical aberration, that was all—an indirect manifestation of how much she loathed him. A shudder of that loathing, surely, and not a shiver of female longing for the touch of a man who epitomised everything that it meant to be a man who could master and command a woman's response whenever he chose to do so. After all, there was no way that she could ever want Vidal. No way at all.

The recognition that her pulse was racing and her heart hammering—with righteous anger, of course—had Fliss pausing to take a calming breath, her hostility towards Vidal momentarily forgotten as she breathed in the magical air of the city. It held her spellbound and entranced. Yes, she could smell petrol and diesel fumes, but more importantly she could also smell air heated by the sun, and infused with something of the historic scents of the East and its once all-powerful Moorish rulers: rich subtle perfumes, aromatic spices. If she closed her eyes Fliss was sure she would be able to hear the musical sound of running water—so beloved of the Moors—and see the rich shimmer of the fabrics that had travelled along the Silk Route to reach Granada.

The historic past of the city seemed to reach out and embrace her—a sigh of sweetly scented breath, a waft of richly erotic perfumes, the sensual touch of silk as fine as the lightest caress.

'This is my car.'

The shock of Vidal's voice intruding on her private thoughts jolted her back to reality, but not quickly enough for her to avoid the hard male hand against her back from which she had already fled. Its heat seemed to sear her skin through her clothes. So might a man such as this one impose his stamp of possession, his mark of ownership on a woman's flesh, imprinting her with that mark for all time. Inside her head an image formed—the image of a male hand caressing the curve of a naked female back. Deliberately and erotically that male hand moved downwards to cup the soft curve of the woman's bottom, turning her to him, his flesh dark against the moonlight paleness of hers, her breathing ragged whilst his deepened into the stalking deliberation of a hunter intent on securing its prey.

No! Her head and her heart were both pounding now as conflicting emotions seized her. She must concentrate on reality. Even knowing that, it still took her a supreme effort of will to do so.

The car he had indicated was very large, very highly polished and black—the kind of car she was used to seeing the rich and powerful being driven around in in London.

'So you aren't a supporter of green issues, then?' Fliss couldn't resist taunting Vidal as he held open the front passenger door of the car for her, taking her small case from her and putting it on the back seat.

The clunk of the door closing was the only response he gave her, before going round to the driver's door and getting into the car himself.

Did his silence mean that she had annoyed and angered him? Fliss hoped so. She *wanted* to get under his skin. She wanted to be a thorn in his side—a reminder to him of what he had done to her, and a reminder to herself.

He hadn't wanted her to come here. She knew that. He had wanted her to simply allow the lawyers to deal with everything. But she had been determined to come. To spite Vidal? No! It was her heritage she sought, not retribution.

The essence of this country ran in her own blood, after all.

Granada—home to the last of the Moorish rulers of the Emirate of Granada and home to the Alhambra, the red fortress, a complex of such great beauty that her mother's face had shone with happiness when she had talked to Fliss about it—was part of her heritage.

'Did my father go there with you?' she had asked her mother.

She had only been seven or so at the time, but she had never referred to the man who had fathered her as 'Daddy'. Daddies were men who played with their children and who loved them— not strangers in a far-off country.

'Yes,' her mother had responded. 'I once took Vidal there, and your father joined us. We had the most lovely day. One day you and I will go there together, Fliss,' her mother had promised.

But somehow that day had never come, so now she was here on her own.

Through the tinted windows of the car she could see the city up ahead of them, its ancient Moorish quarter of Albaicín climbing the hillside that faced the Alhambra. Close to it was the equally historical medieval Jewish quarter of the city, but Fliss wasn't in the least bit surprised, once they were in the city, to find Vidal turning into a street lined with imposing sixteenth-century buildings erected after the city's capture by the Catholic rulers Isabella and Ferdinand. Here on this street the tall Renaissance-style buildings spoke of wealth and privilege, their bulk blotting out the rays of the sun and casting heavy, authoritative shadows.

She might have been surprised to discover that Vidal drove his own car, but she was not surprised when he slowed the car down and then turned in towards a huge pair of imposing double-height studded wooden doors. This area of the city, with its air of arrogance and wealth, was perfectly suited to the man who matched its hauteur—and its visually perfect sculptured classical magnificence.

Fliss was relieved to be distracted from that particular thought by the sight of the sunny courtyard they had just entered, its lines perfectly symmetrical, and even the sound of the water splashing down into the ornate stone fountain in its centre somehow evenly timed.

The house—more a palace, surely, than merely a house—enclosed the courtyard on all four sides, with the main entrance facing the way they had come in. On the wall to their right a two-storey archway led into what had looked like formal gardens from the glimpse Fliss had seen before Vidal had brought the car to a halt alongside a flight of stone steps. The steps led up to a wooden studded door that matched the style of the doors they had just driven through. Around the middle floor of the three-storey building ran what looked like a sort of cloistered, semi-enclosed walkway, whilst the windows looking onto the courtyard were shuttered against the late-afternoon sunlight. On the stonework above the windows Fliss could see the emblem of Granada itself—the pomegranate—whilst above the main doorway were carved what she knew to be the family's arms, along with an inscription which translated as 'What we take we hold'.

It wasn't just the way her job had encouraged her to look at new areas with an eye to their tourism potential that caused her to note these things, Fliss admitted. She had made it her business as she grew up to read as much as she could about the history of Vidal's family—and of course that of her own father.

'Does it ever concern you that this house was built with money stolen from the high-ranking Muslim prince your ancestor murdered?' she challenged Vidal now, determined not to let the beauty and the magnificence of the building undermine her awareness of how the fortune that had bought it had been made.

'There is a saying—to the victor the spoils.

My ancestor was one of many Castilians who won the battle against Boabdil—Muhammad XII—for Ferdinand and Isabella. The money to build this *palacio* was given to him by Isabella, and far from allowing the murder of anyone, the Alhambra Decree treaty gave religious freedome to the city's Muslims.'

'A treaty which was later broken,' Fliss reminded Vidal sharply. 'Just as your ancestor broke the promise he made to the Muslim princess he stole away from her family.'

'My advice to you is that you spend more time checking your supposed facts and rather less repeating them without having done so.'

Without allowing her time to retaliate, Vidal got out of the car, striding so quickly round to the passenger door that Fliss did not have time to open it. Ignoring his outstretched hand, Fliss manoeuvred herself out of the car, determined not to let herself be overwhelmed by her surroundings and instead to think of her mother. Had *she* felt intimidated by the arrogance and the disdain with which this building frowned down upon those who did not belong to it but who were rash enough to enter? Her mother had loved her time in Spain, despite the unhappiness it had eventually brought her. She had been hired by Vidal's parents as an au pair, to help Vidal with his English during the school summer holidays, and she had always made it plain to Fliss just how much she had liked the little boy who had been her charge.

Was it perhaps here in this house that she had first seen and fallen in love with Vidal's adopted uncle—the man who had been her own father? Fliss wondered now. Perhaps she had seen the handsome Spaniard for the first time here in this very courtyard? Handsome, maybe—but not strong enough to stand by her mother and the love he had sworn he felt for her, Fliss reminded herself starkly, lest she get carried away by the romantic imagery created by her surroundings.

She knew that her mother had only visited the

family's house here in Granada very briefly, as most of her time in Spain had been spent at the *castillo* on the ducal country estate, which had been Vidal's parents' main home.

The thought of what her mother must have suffered caused a sensation inside Fliss's chest rather as though iron-hard fingers had closed round her heart and squeezed it—fingers as long and strong as those of Vidal He had played his own part in her mother's humiliation and suffering, Fliss thought bitterly, and she turned quickly away from him—only to give a startled gasp as her foot slipped on one of the cobbles, causing her to turn her ankle and lose her balance.

Immediately the bright sunlight that had been dazzling her was shut out as Vidal stepped towards her, his hands locking round her upper arms as he steadied her and held her upright. Her every instinct was to reject his hold on her, and show him how unwelcome it was. He moved fast, though, releasing her with a look of distaste, as though somehow touching her soiled him.

Anger and humiliation burned inside her, but there was nothing she could do other than turn her back on him. She was trapped—and not just here in a place she did not want to be. She was also trapped by her own past and the role Vidal had played in it. Like the fortress walls with which the Moors had surrounded their cities and their homes, Vidal's contempt for her was a prison from which there was no escape.

Walking past him, Fliss stepped into the building, standing in a cool hallway with a magnificent carved and polished dark wood staircase, to take in the austere and sombre magnificence of her surroundings.

Portraits hung from the white painted walls— stern, uniformed or court-finery-dressed Spanish aristocrats, looking down at her from their heavily gilded frames. Not a single one of them was smiling, Fliss noticed. Rather, they were looking out at the world with expressions of arrogance and disdain. Just as Vidal, their descendant, looked out on the world now.

A door opened to admit a small, plump middle-aged woman with snapping brown eyes that swiftly assessed her. Although she was simply dressed, and not what Fliss had been expecting in Vidal's mother, there was no mistaking her upright bearing and general demeanour of calm confidence.

She realised her assumption was wrong when Vidal announced, 'Let me introduce you to Rosa, who is in charge of the household here. She will show you to your room.'

The housekeeper advanced towards Fliss, her gaze still searching and assessing, and then, ignoring Fliss, she turned back to Vidal. Speaking in Spanish, she told him, 'Where her mother was a dove, this one has the look of a wild falcon not yet tamed to the lure.'

Fresh anger flashed in Fliss's own eyes.

'I speak Spanish,' she told them both. She was almost shaking with the force of her anger. 'And there is no lure that would ever tempt me down into the grasp of anyone in *this* household.'

She just had time to see the answering flash of hostility burn through the look Vidal gave her before she turned on her heel to head towards the stairs, leaving Rosa to come after her.

CHAPTER TWO

ON THE first floor landing Rosa broke the stiff silence between them by saying in a sharp voice, 'So you speak Spanish?'

'Why shouldn't I?' Fliss challenged her. 'No matter what Vidal might want to think, he does not have the power to prevent me from speaking the language that was, after all, my father's native tongue.'

She certainly wasn't going to admit to Rosa, or anyone else here, her early teenage dream of one day meeting her father, which had led to her secretly saving some of her paper-round money to pay for Spanish lessons she'd suspected her mother would not want her to have. Fliss had come to recognise well before she had reached her teens that her mother was almost fearful of

Fliss doing anything to recognise the Spanish side of her inheritance. So, rather than risk upsetting her, Fliss had tried not to let her see how much she had longed to know more about not just her father but his country. Her mother had been a gentle person who had hated confrontations and arguments, and Fliss had loved her far too much to ever want to hurt her.

'Well, you certainly haven't got your spirit from either of your parents,' Rosa told her forthrightly. 'Though I would warn you against trying to cross swords with Vidal.'

Fliss stopped walking, her foot on the first step of the next set of stairs as she turned towards the housekeeper. Her body had immediately tensed with rejection of the thought that she should in any way allow Vidal to control any aspect of her life.

'Vidal has no authority over me,' she told the housekeeper vehemently. 'And he never will have.'

A movement in the hallway below her caught

her attention. She looked back down the stairs and saw that Vidal was still standing there. He must have heard her—which was no doubt the reason for the grim look he was giving her. He probably wished he *did* have some authority over her. If he had he may have prevented her from coming to Spain—just as years ago he had prevented her from making contact with her father.

In her mind's eye she could see him now, standing in her bedroom—the room that should have been her private haven—holding the letter she had sent to her father weeks earlier. A letter which he had intercepted. A letter written from the depths of her sixteen-year-old heart to a father she had longed to know.

Every one of the tenderly burgeoning sensual and emotional feelings she had begun to feel for Vidal had been crushed in that moment. Crushed and turned into bitterness and anger.

'Fliss, darling, you must promise me that you will not attempt to make contact with your father again,' her mother had warned her with tears in her eyes, after Vidal had returned to Spain and it had been just the two of them again.

Of course she had given her that promise. She had loved her mother too much to want to upset her—especially when…

No! She would not allow Vidal to drag her back there, to that searingly shameful place that was burned into her pride for life. Her mother had understood what had happened. She had known Fliss was not to blame.

Maturity had brought her the awareness that, since her father had always known where she was, he could quite easily have made contact with *her* if he'd wished to do so. The fact that he had never done it told its own story. She was not, after all, the only child to grow up not wanted by its father. With her mother's death she had told herself that it was time to move on. Time to celebrate and cherish the childhood and the loving mother she had had, and to forget the father who had rejected her.

She would never know now just what it was that had changed her father's mind. She would never know whether it had been guilt or regret for lost opportunities that had led him to mentioning her in his will. But she did know that this time she was not going to allow Vidal to dictate to her what she could and could not do.

In the hallway below, Vidal watched as Fliss turned on her heel and followed Rosa along the landing to the next flight of stairs. If there was one thing that Vidal prided himself about—one characteristic he had worked on and honed—it was mastery of his own emotions and reactions. But for some reason his gaze—normally so obedient to his command—was finding it necessary to linger on the slender silken length of Fliss's legs as she walked away from him.

At sixteen those legs had been coltishly slender. She had been a child turning into a woman, with pert small breasts that pushed against the thin tee shirts she'd always seemed to wear. She might have behaved towards him with a calculated mock innocence that had involved stolen blushing half-looks, and a wide-eyed pretended inability to lift her supposedly fascinated and awed gaze from the bare expanse of his torso when she had walked into the bathroom whilst he was shaving, but he had witnessed the coarse reality of what she was: promiscuous, and without morals or pride. By nature? Or because she had been deprived of a father?

The guilt he could never escape wrenched at his conscience. How many times over the years had he wished unsaid those innocent words that had led ultimately to the forced ending of the relationship between his uncle and his au pair? A simple mention to his grandmother that Felipe had joined them on an expedition to the Alhambra here in Granada had been their undoing—and his.

There had been no way that the Dowager Duchess would ever have allowed Felipe to marry anyone other than a woman of her choice.

Nor would she ever have chosen a mere au pair as a bride for a man whose blood was as aristocratic as that of his adoptive family.

As a child of seven Vidal had not understood that, but he had quickly realised the consequences of his innocent actions when he had been told that the gentle English au pair of whom he had become so fond was being dismissed and sent home. Neither Fliss's mother nor Felipe had had natures strong enough to challenge his grandmother's authority. Neither of them had known when they were forced to part that there would be consequences to their love in the form of the child Fliss's mother had conceived. A child whose name and very existence his grandmother had ruled was never to be mentioned—unless she herself did so, in order to remind his uncle of the shame he had brought on his adoptive family by lowering himself to conceive that child with a mere au pair.

How justified his grandmother would have believed her ruling to be had she lived long enough to know what Felipe's daughter had become.

Vidal had felt for Felicity's mother when the two of them had returned early from a visit to London to discuss various private matters to find that not only was Felicity having an illicit teenage party that had got badly out of hand, but also that Felicity herself was upstairs in her mother's bedroom with a drunken, ignorant lout of a youth.

Vidal closed his eyes and then opened them again. There were some memories he preferred not to revisit. The realisation that he had inadvertently betrayed his au pair's love affair. The night his mother had come into his room to tell him that the plane his father had been in had crashed in South America without any survivors. The evening he had looked at Felicity sprawled on her mother's bed, her gold and honey-streaked blonde hair wrapped round the hand of the youth leaning over her, whilst she stared up at him with brazen disregard for what she had done.

Brazen disregard for *him*.

Vidal's chest lifted under the demanding pressure of his lungs for oxygen. He had been twenty-three—a man, not a boy—and appalled by the effect Felicity was having on him. Revolted by the desire he felt for her, tormented by both it and his own moral code—a code that said that a girl of sixteen was just that—a *girl*—and a man of twenty-three was also exactly that—a *man*. The seven-year age gap between them was a gap that separated childhood from adulthood, and represented a chasm that must not be violated. Just as a sixteen-year-old's innocence must not be violated.

Even now, seven years later, he could still taste the anger that had soured his heart and seared his soul. A bleak black burning anger that Felicity's presence here was re-igniting.

Vidal flexed the tense muscles of his shoulders. The sooner this whole business was over and done with and Felicity was on a plane on her way back to the UK the better.

When Felipe had been dying, and had told him how badly he felt about the past, Vidal had encouraged him to make reparation via his will to the child he had fathered and then been forced to abandon. He had done that for his uncle's sake, though—not for Felicity's.

Upstairs in the room Rosa had shown her into, before telling her that refreshments would be sent up for her and then leaving, Fliss studied her surroundings. The room was vast, with a high ceiling, and furnished with heavy and ornate dark wood furniture of a type that Fliss knew from her mother's descriptions was typical in expensive antique Spanish furniture. Beautifully polished, and without a speck of dust, the wood glowed warmly in the light pouring in through the room's tall French windows. Stepping up to them, Fliss saw that they opened out onto a small balcony, decorated with waist-high beautifully intricate metalwork, its design classically Arabic rather than European. Try as she might,

Fliss could not spot the deliberate flaw that was always said to be made in such work, because only Allah himself could create perfection.

The balcony looked down on an equally classical Moorish courtyard garden, bisected by the straight lines of the rill of water that flowed through it from a fall spilling out of some concealed source at the far end of the courtyard. Either side of the narrow canal were covered walkways smothered in soft pink climbing roses, their scent rising up to the balcony. On the ground alongside them were white lilies. The pathways themselves were made from subtle blue and white tiles, whilst what looked like espaliered fruit trees lined the walls of the courtyard. In the four small square formal gardens on the opposite side of the rose walkways, white geraniums tumbled from Ali Baba–sized terracotta jars, whilst directly below the balcony, partly shaded from the sun by a sort of cloistered, semi-enclosed area, there was a patio complete with elegant garden furniture.

Fliss closed her eyes. She knew this garden so well. Her mother had described it to her, sketched it for her, shown her photographs of it. She had told her that it was a garden originally designed for the exclusive use of the women of the Moorish family for whom the house had been built. It was obviously an act of deliberate cruelty on the part of Vidal to have given her this room, overlooking the garden he knew her mother had loved so much. Had he given her the room her mother had slept in? Fliss suspected that he hadn't. Her mother had told her that she and Vidal had occupied the top storey—the nursery quarters—when they had come to stay with Vidal's grandmother, who in those days had owned the house, even though Vidal had been seven years old at the time.

Fliss turned back into the room. Heavily embossed with a raised self-coloured pattern, a rich deep blue brocade fabric hung at the windows and covered the straight-backed chairs placed at either side of the room's marble fireplace.

The cream bedspread was piped in the same blue, with tasselled blue brocade cushions ornamenting its immaculate cream width. The dark wooden floorboards shone, and the antique-looking blue-and-cream rug that covered most of the floor was so plush that Fliss felt she hardly dared walk on it.

It was all a far cry from her minimalist apartment back at home. But this decor just as much as the decor she had chosen for herself was a part of her genetic inheritance through her father. Had he not rejected her mother, had he not denied them both, she would have grown up familiar with this house and its history, taking it for granted. Just as Vidal himself did.

Vidal. How she loathed him. Her feelings towards him were far more bitter and filled with contempt than her feelings towards her father. Her father, after all, had had no voice. As her mother had explained to her, he had been forced to give them up and to turn his back on them. *He* had not opened her letter pleading to be given a chance to get to know him and then told her that she must never ever try to contact him again. Vidal had done that. *He* had never known her personally and looked at her with a gaze of cold contempt, then rejected her and walked away from her, as Vidal had done. *He* had never scorched her pride and burned a wound deep into her heart with his misjudgement of her. Vidal had.

It was here in this house that decisions had been made. They had impacted on her and on her parents in the most cruel way. It was from here that her mother had been dismissed. It was here that she had been told that the man she loved was promised in marriage to another—a girl chosen for him by his adoptive family, who was in her final year at an exclusive school that groomed highly born girls for their marriages. A girl, as her mother had told Fliss, Felipe had sworn to her he did not love and certainly did not want to marry.

It hadn't mattered what Felipe wanted, though.

All his promises to Fliss's mother, all his pro-
testations of love, had been as beads of light
caused by the sun's rays touching the drops of
water as they fell from a fountain. So beautiful
and entrancing that they stopped the heart, but
ephemeral and insubstantial when it came to
reality.

There had only been time for the two of them
to snatch a final goodbye embrace and share the
fevered illicit intimacy that had led to her own
conception before they had been torn apart—
her mother sent back to England and Felipe instructed to do his duty and propose to the girl
who had been chosen for him.

'He swore to me that he loved me, but he loved
his adoptive family too and he could not disobey
them,' her mother had told her gently, when she
had asked as a girl why he had not come after
her.

Her poor mother. She had made the mistake
of falling in love with a man who had not been
strong enough to protect their love, and she had

paid the price for that. Fliss would never let the same thing happen to her. She would never allow herself to fall in love and be vulnerable. After all, she had already had a taste of how that felt—even if her feelings for Vidal had merely been those of an inexperienced sixteen-year-old.

Shaking herself free of her painful thoughts, she looked at her small case. Her mother had told her about the traditional way of life of this aristocratic, autocratic Spanish family that Vidal now headed. Vidal had said that his mother had insisted she stay here. Did that mean she could expect to be formally received by her? Perhaps over dinner? She hadn't brought any formal clothes with her—just a few changes of under-wear, a pair of tailored shorts, some fresh tops, and one very simple slip of a dress: a handful of non-crushable matt black jersey that she had fallen in love with on a trip to London.

She was just about to lift the dress from her case and shake it out when the door opened and

Rosa came in, carrying a tray containing a glass of wine and a serving of tapas.

After thanking her, Fliss asked, 'What time is dinner served?'

'There will be no dinner. Vidal does not wish it. He is too busy,' Rosa answered haughtily in Spanish. 'A meal will be brought for you if you wish.'

Fliss could feel her face beginning to burn. Rosa's rudeness was unforgivable—but no doubt she was taking her cue from Vidal.

'I have no more wish to eat with Vidal than he does with me,' she told Rosa spiritedly. 'But since Vidal told me specifically that it was his mother's wish that I stay here, instead of in the hotel I had booked, I assumed I would be expected to have dinner with *her.*'

'The Duchess is not here,' Rosa informed her curtly, putting down the tray and turning grim-lipped to the door. She had disappeared through it before Fliss could ask her any more questions.

Vidal had lied to her about his mother's presence here in the house and about her wish to see her. Why? Why would he want to have her here beneath his own roof?

Just for a moment she wished she was back at home—and more than that she wished that her mother was still alive. Filled with the sadness of her emotions, Fliss sat down on the edge of the bed.

Her mother had given her the best childhood ever. A wonderfully generous bequest of an elderly relative Fliss herself had never even known had enabled her mother to buy them a lovely home in a quiet country village—large enough for Fliss's grandparents to move in with them— as well as providing an income which had meant her mother had been able to be at home with her. Her mother had talked openly to her about her father, referring to him with love in her voice and her eyes, and no resentment or bitterness. She had only clammed up when Fliss had begged her to bring her to Spain so that she could see the country for herself. She had refused to criticise Vidal when Fliss, with a seven-year-old's sharpness of mind, had worked out that *he* must have been the one to betray her parents.

'You mustn't blame Vidal, darling,' her mother had told her gently. 'It truly wasn't his fault. He was only a little boy—the same age as you are now. He was not to know what would happen.'

Her gentle, loving mother—always so ready to understand and forgive those who hurt her.

Initially Felicity—named for 'happiness', according to her mother—had accepted this defence of Vidal. But then he had come to visit them, and after initially behaving towards her with kindness he had started to treat her with disdain, putting as much distance between them as he could, and making it plain that he disliked her. How her vulnerable teenage heart had ached over that unkindness.

From the minute she had first seen him, stepping out of the expensive car he had driven from London to their house, Fliss had been smitten, developing a huge crush on him. She could vividly remember the day she had inadvertently walked into the bathroom when he had been shaving. Her besotted gaze had been glued to his naked torso. Of course that kind of intimacy had sent her febrile teenage longings surging out of control. Theirs had normally been a mostly female household, so the sight of any bare male chest would have had her studying it in secret curiosity, but when that bare chest belonged to Vidal…

She had felt almost sick with excitement and longing when she had finally managed to step back out of the bathroom, her imagination working overtime and conjuring up various scenarios in which she had not merely looked at it but even more breathtakingly excitingly been held close to it. It was all very well to mock her sixteen-year-old naivety now, but wasn't it the truth that she was still every bit as personally unfamiliar with the actual reality of sexual intimacy, bare skin to bare skin, now as she had been then?

Clumsily Fliss turned round, as though in flight from her own knowledge of herself. But the fact was that there was nowhere to run to from the reality of her virgin state. No matter how many defensive barricades she had built around herself, no matter how strong an aura of adult womanly confidence she had taught herself to manifest, and no matter how closely she guarded the secret of her past-its-sell-by-date virginity, she could not escape from the truth.

What was the matter with her? she challenged herself. She had lived with being sexually inactive for years. It had been her own decision to make and to keep. It was just one of those things. The pace of modern life, the need to establish her career, had somehow prevented her from meeting a man she wanted enough to let go of the past.

It would be pure self-indulgence for her to start feeling sorry for herself. By many people's standards Fliss knew that her childhood had been a privileged one. She still considered herself to be privileged now—and not just because she had had such a wonderful mother.

With her grandparents and her mother dead, the big house had seemed so empty—and yet at the same time filled with painful memories. At the height of the property market, before it crashed, Fliss had been approached by a builder who had offered her an unexpectedly large sum of money for the house and its land. After trying to work out what her mother would have wanted her to do she had gone ahead and sold the house to him, and bought herself the flat in the converted Georgian townhouse. Her work in the Tourism Department of the very pretty market town in which she lived kept her busy, and she had plenty of friends—although many of her schoolfriends were now pairing off and making 'nesting' plans, and her three closest friends from school and university, whilst single like her, now lived and worked overseas.

A brief rap on her bedroom door had her getting up off the bed and tensing as she waited for the door to open and Rosa to appear—no doubt radiating further disapproval.

However, it wasn't Rosa who stepped or rather strode into the room, but Vidal himself. He had changed from his business suit into a more casual shirt and a pair of chinos, and had also had a shower, to judge from the still-damp appearance of his slicked-back hair. Her heart turned over inside her chest cavity in slow painful motion, her breath seizing in her lungs. Her awareness of the intimacy of him being in her bedroom brought back too many memories of the past for her to feel comfortable even before the door had closed and locked.

Once before Vidal had come into her bedroom…

No! She would not allow herself to be dragged into the dark agony of that dreadful place where those memories were stored. It was the present she needed to focus on—not the past. It was she who must challenge and criticise Vidal—not the other way around.

Summoning her strength, she demanded, 'Why did you tell me that your mother would be here when that was a lie?'

The sudden surge of blood creeping up along his jaw betrayed his real reaction to her challenge, even if he was trying to deny it by giving her a coolly dismissive look.

'My mother has been called away to visit a friend who is unwell. I was not aware of her absence myself until Rosa informed me of it.'

'Rosa had to tell you where your mother is? How typical of the kind of man you are that you need a servant to tell you the whereabouts of your own mother.'

The hot, angry red blood surged over the sharp thrust of his jawline like an unstoppable tide.

'For your information, Rosa is *not* a servant. And as for my relationship with my mother—that is not a subject I intend to discuss with you.'

'No, I'm sure you don't,' Fliss answered him grimly. 'After all, it is in no small part because of you that I never got to have a relationship with my *father*. You were the one who intercepted my private letter to him. And you were the one who came all the way to England to bully my mother into pleading with me not to try to contact him again.'

'Your mother believed it would not have been in your best interests for you to continue to write to Felipe.'

'Oh, so it was for *my* sake that you stopped me communicating with him, was it?' Fliss's voice was icy with sarcasm as the memory of all the anguish and humiliation Vidal had caused flooded past her defences. He was cruel and arrogant. Willing to destroy others without compunction so that he could have his own way. 'You had no right to stop me knowing my father, or denying me the right to at least see if he could love me. But then we know that love for another person isn't a concept someone like you understands, is it, Vidal?'

She could feel the aching burn of her emotions in the hot tears that threatened to flood her eyes.

Tears! She would never—*must* never—ever cry in front of this man. She must never show him any weakness. *Never.*

'What could you possibly know about loving someone—about loving *anyone*?' Fliss hurled accusations at him in furious self-defence. She'd say and do anything to stop him guessing at the pain within her that his words had touched. 'You don't know what love is!'

She had no idea what she was really saying as the wild words tumbled from her lips. All she knew was that they sprang from an unending well of pain deep inside her.

'And you *do*? You who—' Furiously angry himself, Vidal closed the distance between them, shaking his head in disgust as he stopped speaking.

But Fliss knew perfectly what he had been about to say, and the accusation he had been about to fling at her.

Now panic as well as pain had her well and truly in its grip

'Don't touch me,' she ordered, stepping back from him, her voice shaking with dread.

'You can stop the play-acting, Felicity.' Immediately Vidal's anger was replaced by a look of contempt. 'And we both know that it *is* play-acting, before you attempt to deny it and perjure yourself even further.'

Her panic levels were going through the roof, sky-high and out of control, defeating her as she struggled to bring some rationality to her reactions and her emotions.

The memories had come dangerously close, muddying the waters of what was present and what was past. Her heart was jumping around inside her ribcage and she was sixteen years old again, floundering helplessly at the confusion of feelings that were forbidden and frightening.

'I know what you're thinking,' she lashed out wildly, 'but you're wrong. I don't want you. I never wanted you.'

'Want me?'

The silence in the room was like the still centre

at the eye of a storm. It was like knowing with all her senses that the danger was there and soon it would crash down on her and consume her. And there was nowhere she could run to escape it.

'Want me? Like this, you mean?' Vidal said softly.

'This' was being ruthlessly dragged into his arms and then being pinioned against him, trapped between him and the wall behind her, as he bound her to his body so intimately that she felt as though she could feel the bones and the hard male muscles that lay beneath the sleek flesh that padded them. Unlike her own, his heartbeat was steady—steady and determined. The heartbeat of a victor who had successfully captured his prey.

Was this how that long-ago Moorish princess had felt held in the vice-like grip of her captor?

Fliss's own heartbeat raced, her pulse flickering in a wild primeval dance that took away her ability to think or even feel rationally. Had she, that long-ago young woman, also felt the same searing, soaring, confusing of fear and triumph? Fear for her independence—fear of the wild clamouring that was beating through her. And had she felt triumph because she had been able to drive the man holding her beyond his own self-control? Because she had broken something in him? Even though the price of that victory would be him exerting his power over her in retaliation?

A mêlée of thoughts and feelings rioted inside her, turning her into a version of herself she barely recognised.

He shouldn't be doing this, Vidal knew, but somehow he couldn't stop himself. A thousand nights and more of dragging himself from forbidden dreams in which he held her like this overwhelmed his self-control. She wasn't sixteen any more; she wasn't forbidden by his own moral code—even if his pride burned and recoiled at the thought of still desiring her.

The girl with the wide-eyed gaze, filled with all the heady innocence of a sixteen-year-old in the grip of her first sexual desire for a man, had never existed anywhere other than in his imagination. All the nights he had lain sleepless and tormented the bed *she* had been lying in had been far from chaste.

As he bent his head towards hers he could feel the thud of her heartbeat and the soft warmth of her breasts pressed against his chest—those breasts from which he had ached so badly to peel the tee shirt covering them so that he could reveal their perfection to his gaze and touch, so that he could pluck on the tormenting thrust of her nipples with his fingertips, so that he could draw them into his mouth and caress them until her body arched with longing for his possession.

No! He must not do this.

Vidal made to release her, but Fliss shuddered violently against him, the small sound she made deep in her throat drowning out his denial.

Vidal was looking into her eyes, forcing her to

look back at him. Close up, his eyes weren't one solid colour but several shades mingling together into topaz-gold. The unblinking intensity of his gaze was dizzying her, just as the heavy thud of his heart beating was commanding her own heart to match its rhythm.

In another heartbeat he would kiss her, and she would feel the cold, unforgiving dominance of those sharply cut lips. Her own parted—on a protest against what he was doing, not a sign of her docile acceptance of it, and certainly not in eager anticipation of it.

And yet…

And yet beneath her clothes, beneath her top and her plain, practical neutral-coloured bra, her breasts had begun to ache with a sensation that seemed to have spread down from where his hand was covering the pulse in her throat to the tightening peaks of her nipples. Fliss trembled in its grip, shockingly forced to admit to herself that what her body and that ache within it was signalling was *not* angry rejection. Instead a burgeoning female desire was running through her veins like heavy, melting liquid pleasure—a pleasure that lapped at her senses and undermined her self-control, replacing it with a growing sensual longing.

Vidal's breath grazed her skin, clean and slightly minty. Beneath the newly cleansed scent of his skin her senses picked up something else—something primitive and dangerous to a woman whose own sensuality had broken past the barriers of her self-control. The scent of alluring raw maleness, which called out to that sensuality and somehow had her moving closer to him, her lips parting just a little bit more.

Their gazes clung and fought hotly for supremacy, and then his mouth was on hers. The pressure of those male lips was sending her senses into overdrive, causing a heat explosion of pleasure to melt liquid desire into her lower body.

Fliss tried to fight what she was feeling. She made a helpless sound—she could feel it reverberating in her own throat—a sound of protest,

Fliss was sure. Although her ears translated it more as a shockingly keening moan of need. A need that was instantly increased by the insistent grind of Vidal's body into her own, and a tightening of his hold on her whilst his tongue took possession of the intimate softness of her mouth, thrusting against her own tongue, taking her to a place of dark velvet sensuality and danger. Her whole body was on fire, pulsing with a reaction to him which seemed to have exploded inside her. Her eyes closed...

Vidal felt the force of his own angry desire surging through him, sweeping aside barriers within himself he had thought impenetrable. The more he tried to regain control, the more savage his reaction became. Anger and out-of-control male desire. Each of them was dangerous enough alone, but incite them both, as this woman he was holding now had done, and the alchemic reaction between them had the power to rip a man's self-respect to shreds—and with it his belief in himself.

Behind his own closed eyelids Vidal saw her as his body most wanted her: naked, eager to appease the male passion she had induced and unleashed, offering herself. Her white skin would be pearlescent with the dew of her own arousal, the dark pink crests of her breasts flowering into hard nubs of pleasure that sought the caress of his fingertips and his lips.

Outside in the garden below them the gathering dusk activated the system that brought on the garden lighting. Sudden illumination burst into life, causing Vidal to open his eyes and recognise what he was doing.

Cursing himself mentally, he released Fliss abruptly.

The shock of transition from a kiss so intimate that she felt it had seared her senses for ever to the reality of who exactly had been delivering that kiss had Fliss shuddering with self-revulsion. But before she could gather her scattered senses—before she could do anything, before she could tell Vidal what she thought of him—he was speaking to her. As though what he had done had never happened.

'What I came to tell you is that it will be an early start in the morning, since we have a ten-o'clock appointment with your father's lawyer. Rosa will send someone up with your breakfast, since my mother isn't expected back until tomorrow. I also have to tell you that any future attempt by you to…to *persuade* me to satisfy your promiscuously carnal desires will be as doomed to failure as this one.' His mouth twisted cynically and he gave her a coldly insulting look. 'Over-used goods have never held any appeal for me.'

Over-used goods.

Trembling with rage at his insult, Fliss lost her head. 'You were the one who started this, not me. And…and you're wrong about me. You always have been. What you saw—'

'What I saw was a sixteen-year-old tramp, lying on her mother's bed, allowing a young lout to paw her and boast that *he* intended to have her because the rest of his football team already had.'

'Get out!' Fliss demanded, her voice rising in anger. 'Get *out*!'

He strode away from her and through the bedroom door.

As soon as she could trust herself to move she half ran and half stumbled to the door, turning the key in the lock, tears of rage and shame spilling from her hot eyes.

CHAPTER THREE

IT WAS too late to try and hold back the memories now. They were there with her in every raw and cruel detail.

Fliss sank down into one of the chairs, her head in her hands.

She had been shocked and hurt when Vidal had told her that he'd intercepted her letter to her father. Such a cruel action from someone she had put on a pedestal had hurt very badly, coming on top of Vidal's existing coldness towards her. Rejection by her father and his family—something she had always tried to pretend didn't matter—had suddenly become very real and very painful. She had seen the warmth with which Vidal treated her mother, and that had made her own sense of rejection worse. He wasn't after being cold to them both—just to her.

When her mother had told her that Vidal was taking her out to dinner as a thank-you for his stay, Fliss had asked if she might have some schoolfriends round to celebrate the ending of the school year and their exams. Her mother had agreed—on the strict understanding that she was only to invite half a dozen of her class-mates. This had seemed fair to Fliss and so she had been horrified when their get-together was interrupted by the arrival of what had seemed like dozens of teenagers—many of whom already the worse for drink.

She had tried to persuade them to leave, but her efforts had been met by jeers and even more rowdy behaviour. One of the boys—Rory—had been the ringleader of a wild crowd from her school. A swaggering bully of a boy who'd played in the school football team. He had gone upstairs with the girl who had arrived with him—a stranger to Fliss—and she had followed them, horrified when they went into her mother's bedroom.

In the row that had followed the girl had left, and Rory, furious with Fliss, who had been 'spoiling his fun', had grabbed her and pulled her down onto the bed. His actions had turned Fliss's anger to fear. She had tried to pull free and fight him off, but he had laughed at her, pouring cider over her from the bottle he had brought up with him and then pushing her back against the bed.

That was when the door had opened and she had seen her mother and Vidal standing there. At first she had been relieved—but then she had seen the look on Vidal's face. So had Rory, because that had been when he had made that crude and completely untrue comment about the rest of the football team, followed by an equally untrue statement.

'She loves it. She can't get enough of it. Ask any of the lads. They all know how well she's up for it. A proper little nympho, she is.'

Fliss could still remember the feeling of shocked disbelief icing through her, making it impossible for her to speak or move; to defend herself or refute his boast. Instead she had simply lain there, numbed with horror, whilst Vidal had pulled Rory from the bed and marched him downstairs.

Her mother's shocked, 'Oh, Fliss…' had been ringing in her ears as she'd followed.

Later, of course, she had explained what had happened to her mother, and thankfully her mother had believed her, but by that time Vidal had been on his way back to Spain, and the pain she had felt on seeing the contempt and loathing in his eyes as he'd looked at her had turned her crush on him into revulsion and anger.

She had never gone back to school. She and the three girls who had become her closest friends had gone instead to a sixth-form college, thanks to the excellence of their exam results, and Fliss had made a private vow to herself that she would make her mother proud of her. She would never, ever allow another man to look at her as Vidal had done. She had never discussed with anyone just what his misjudgement of her that evening had done to her. It was her private shame. And now Vidal had resurrected that shame.

Downstairs in the library, with its high ceiling and Biblical frescoes, Vidal stood motionless and white-lipped, staring unseeingly into space, oblivious to the grandeur of his surroundings. The bookshelves were laden with leather-covered books, their titles painted on the spines in gold, and the scent of leather and paper pervaded the room.

Vidal knew himself to be a man of strong principle, with deep passions and convictions about his ancestry and his duty to it, and to the people who depended on him. Never before had the strength of those passions boiled over into the fury that Felicity had aroused in him. Never before had he come so close to having his self-control consumed in such intense fires.

If he hadn't been stopped when those lights had come on…

He would have stopped anyway, he assured himself. But a critical inner voice demanded silkily, *Would you?* Or would he have continued to be consumed by his own out-of-control emotions until he had had Felicity spread naked on the bed beneath him, as he sought to satisfy the hunger within him he had thought extinguished?

Vidal closed his eyes and then opened them again. He had thought he'd put the past behind him, but Felicity had brought it back to life with a vengeance.

He needed this to be over. He needed to walk away from the past and draw a line under it. He needed to be rid of it—and for that to happen he needed to be rid of Felicity herself.

Vidal's mouth compressed. As soon as they had seen Felipe's lawyer, and arrangements had been made for Vidal to buy from Felicity the house her father had left her, he would remove her from his life—permanently.

* * *

Upstairs in the bathroom adjoining her bedroom, the door safely locked, Fliss stood motionless and dry-eyed beneath the beating lash of the powerful shower. She was beyond tears, beyond anger—except for the anger that burned inside her against herself—beyond anything other than the knowledge that she could stand beneath the fiercely drumming water for the rest of her life— but no amount of water would ever wash away the stain she herself had stamped—dyed—into her pride via what she had done when she had responded to Vidal's contemptuous kiss.

Stepping out of the shower, she reached for a towel. Perhaps she should not have come here, after all. But that was what Vidal had wanted, wasn't it? The letter he had sent as her father's executor, advising her of the fact that her father had left her his house, had said that there was no need. No need as far as *he* was concerned, but every need for her, Fliss reminded herself as she towelled her hair dry. Her body was concealed from her own gaze by the thick soft towel she had wrapped around herself, which covered her from her breasts down to her feet. She had no wish to look upon the flesh that had betrayed her. Or was she the one who had betrayed it? Had she had more experience, more lovers, the lifestyle and the men Vidal had accused her of giving herself to—if she had not deliberately refused to allow her sexuality and her sensuality to know the pleasures they were made for—she would surely have been better equipped to deal with what was happening to her now.

She couldn't possibly *really* have wanted Vidal. That was impossible.

Her heart started to beat jerkily, so that she had to put her hand over it in an attempt to calm it.

It *was* impossible, wasn't it? A woman would have to be bereft of all pride and self-protection to allow herself to feel any kind of desire for a man who had treated her as Vidal had. It was the past that was doing this to her—trapping her, refusing to let her move forward. The past and the unhealed wounds Vidal had inflicted on her there…

It was the sound of her bedroom door rattling that brought Fliss out of the uneasy sleep she had eventually fallen into, after what had felt like hours of lying awake with her body tense and her mind a whirlwind of angry, passionate thoughts. At first the image conjured up inside her head was one of Vidal, his long fingers curled round the door handle. Immediately a surge of sensation burned through her body, igniting an unfamiliar and unwanted sensual ache that shocked her into reality—and shame.

The darkness of the night, with its sensually tempting whispers and torments, was over. It was morning now. Light and sunshine flooded into the room through the windows over which she had forgotten to close the curtains the previous night.

The faint knocking she could still hear on the

door was far too hesitant to come from a man like Vidal.

Calling out that she would unlock the door, Fliss got out of bed, glad that she had done so when she discovered a small, nervous-looking young maid standing outside the door and pushing a trolley containing Fliss's breakfast.

Thanking her, Fliss quickly checked her watch. It was gone eight o'clock already, and her appointment with her late father's lawyer was at ten. She had no idea where the offices were, or how long it would take to get there. She'd have preferred to go there alone, but of course with Vidal named as her late father's executor that was impossible.

With the maid gone, Fliss gulped down a few swallows of the deliciously fragrant coffee she had poured for her, and snatched small bites from one of the fresh warm rolls which she had broken open and spread with sharp orange conserve. Her mother had told her about this special orange conserve, beloved of the family, which was made with the oranges from their own groves. Just tasting it reminded her of her mother, and that in turn helped to calm her and steady her resolve.

Half an hour later she was showered and dressed in a clean tee shirt and her plain dark 'city' skirt, her hair brushed back off her face and confined in a clip in a way that unwittingly revealed the delicacy of her features and the slender length of her neck. Fliss automatically touched the small heart-shaped gold locket that hung from her neck on its narrow gold chain. It had been a gift from her father to her mother. Her mother had worn it always, and now Fliss wore it in her memory.

A swift curl of mascara and a slick of lipstick and she was ready. And just in time, she reflected as she heard another knock on her bedroom door—a rather more confident one this time. When she opened the bedroom door it was to find Rosa standing outside, her expression as wary and disapproving as it had been the previous evening.

'You are to go down to the library. I will show you the way,' she announced in Spanish, her button-shiny, sharp dark eyes assessing Fliss in a way that made Fliss feel her appearance had been found wanting when compared with the elegance no doubt adopted by the kind of women a man like Vidal preferred. Soignée, sophisticated, designer-clad women with that air of cool hauteur and reserve her mother had told her that highborn Spanish women wore like the all-covering muslin robes once worn by the Moors who had preceded them.

So what? She was here to speak with her father's lawyers, not to dress to impress a man who filled her with dislike and contempt, Fliss reminded herself.

No sound other than that made by their feet on the stairs broke the heavy silence of the house's dark interior as Rosa escorted her down to the library, opening the door for her and telling her briskly that she was to wait inside for Vidal.

Normally Fliss would have been unable to resist looking at the titles of the books filling the double-height shelves that ran round the whole room, but for some reason she felt too on edge to do anything other than wish that the coming meeting was safely over.

Safely over? Why should she feel unsafe and on edge? She already knew the contents of her father's will so far as they concerned her. He had left Fliss the house he himself had inherited from Vidal's grandmother, on the ducal estate in the Lecrin Valley, along with a small sum of money, whilst the agricultural land that surrounded it had been returned to the main estate.

Was she wrong to feel that there was a message for her in this bequest? Was it just her own long-ing that made her hope it was the loving touch of a father filled with regret for a relationship never allowed to exist? Was it foolish of her to yearn somehow to find something of what might have been? Some shadowy ghost of regret to warm her heart, waiting for her in the home her father had left her?

Fliss knew that if Vidal were to guess what she was thinking he would destroy her fragile hopes and leave her with nothing to soften the rejection of her childhood years. Which was why he must not know why she had come here, instead of staying in England as he instructed her to do. In the house where her father had lived she might finally find something to ease the pain she had grown up with. After all, her father must have intended *something* by leaving her his home. An act like that was in its own way an act of love, and she longed so much to have that love.

Not that she couldn't help wishing the house was somewhere other than so close to Vidal's family *castillo*.

As grand as this townhouse was, Fliss knew from her mother that it couldn't compare with the magnificence of the ducal *castillo*, in the idyllically beautiful Lecrin Valley to the south of Granada.

Set on the south-westerly slopes of the Sierra Nevada, and running down to the coast with its sub-tropical climate, the valley had been much loved by the Moors, who had spoken of the area as the Valley of Happiness. Her mother's voice had been soft with emotion when she had told Fliss that in spring the air was filled with the scent of the blossom from the orchards that surrounded the castle.

Olives, almonds, cherries, and wine from the vines that covered many acres of its land were produced in abundance by the ducal estate, and the house owned by her father was, Fliss knew, called House of Almond Blossom because it was set amongst an orchard of those trees.

Was Vidal trying to undermine her in having her brought to this so openly male-orientated room and then left here alone, virtually imprisoned in its austere and unwelcoming maleness? she questioned, her thoughts returning to the present. Why couldn't Rosa have simply called her down when Vidal himself was ready to leave for the lawyer's office? Why had she been made to wait here, in this room that spoke so forcefully of male power and male arrogance?

As though her hostile thoughts had somehow conjured him up, the door swung open and Vidal stepped into the room—just as she was in angry, agitated mid-pace, her eyes flashing telltale signs of what she was feeling as she looked towards him.

He was dressed in a pair of narrow black chinos that hugged the litheness of his hips and stretched with the movement of his thighs, drawing her treacherous gaze to the obvious strength and power of the male muscles there. As though having already been accused and found guilty of treachery, and deciding that it now had nothing left to lose, her gaze moved boldly upwards, its awareness of him unhampered by the white shirt covering the physical reality of his torso.

Aghast, Fliss realised that her imagination had

joined in the betrayal and was now supplying her with totally unwanted images of what lay beneath that shirt—right down to providing her with a mental picture of every single powerful muscle his flesh cloaked from the memories her senses had stored after her proximity to him last night.

Only when her gaze reached his throat was Fliss finally able to drag it back down to the shiny polished gleam of his shoes as it quailed at the thought of daring to rest on his mouth, or meet the gaze of those topaz-gold eyes.

She felt slightly breathless, and her senses were quivering—with distaste and dislike, Fliss insisted to herself. Not with awareness or—perish the thought—some horrible and unwanted surge of female desire.

Her heart started pounding far too heavily, the sound drumming inside her own head like a warning call. Her lips had started to burn. She desperately wanted to lick them—to cool them down, to impose the feel of her own tongue against them and wipe away the memory of Vidal's kiss. So much treachery from her own body. Where had it come from, and why? She tried to think of her father and remind herself of why she was here, dredging up the broken strands of her self-control from the whirlpool into which they had been sucked.

Taking a deep breath, she told Vidal, 'It's nearly ten o'clock. I seem to remember that last night you warned me against being late for our appointment with the lawyer—but apparently that same rule does not apply to you.'

He was frowning now, obviously disliking the fact that she had dared to question him. His voice was cool and sharp as he answered. 'As you say, it's nearly ten o'clock—but since Señor Gonzales has not yet arrived, so far as I am concerned I am ahead of time.'

'The lawyer is coming *here*?' Fliss demanded, ignoring his attack on her. Her face flamed like that of a child caught out in a social solecism, or a *faux pas*. Of *course* a man as aristocratic and as arrogant as Vidal would expect lawyers to attend him—not the other way round.

The loud pealing of a bell echoing through the marble-floored hallway beyond the half-open library door silenced any further comment Fliss might have tried to make.

No doubt feeling that he had triumphed over her, Vidal strode away from her. Fliss could hear him greeting and welcoming another man, whose voice she could also now hear.

'Coffee in the library, please, Rosa,' Fliss heard Vidal instructing the housekeeper as the two men approached the open doorway.

She had no real reason to feel apprehensive or even nervous, but she *did* feel both those emotions, Fliss admitted as Vidal waved the small dark-suited man who must be Señor Gonzales into the library ahead of him, and then introduced him to her.

The lawyer gave her an old-fashioned and formal half-bow, before extending his hand to shake hers.

'Señor Gonzales will go through the terms of your late father's will in so far as they relate to you. As was explained to you in the letter I sent, as your father's executor it is part of my role to carry out his wishes.'

As he led them over to the imposing dark wood desk at one side of the room's marble fireplace, Fliss recognised that note in Vidal's voice that said there had been no need for her to come to Spain to hear what had already been reported to her via letter, but Fliss refused to be undermined by it. The lawyer, polite though he had been to her, was bound to be on Vidal's side, she warned herself, and she would have to be on her guard with both of them.

'My late father has left me his house. I know that,' Fliss agreed once they were all seated round the desk. She broke off from what she was saying when a maid came in with the coffee, which had to be poured and handed out to them with due formality before they were alone again.

'Felipe wanted to make amends to you for the fact that he had not been able to acknowledge you formally and publicly whilst he was alive,' Señor Gonzales said quietly.

Silently Fliss digested his words.

'Financially—'

'Financially I have no need of my father's inheritance,' Fliss interrupted him quickly.

She was *not* going to allow Vidal to think even worse of her than he already did and suggest that it was the financial aspect of her inheritance that had brought her here. The truth was that she would far rather have had a personal letter from her father proclaiming his love for her than any amount of money.

'Thanks to the generosity of one of my English relatives my mother and I never suffered financially from my father's rejection of us. My mother's great aunt did not reject us. She thought enough of us to want to help us. She cared when others did not.'

Fliss felt proud to be able to point out to the

two men that it was her mother's family who had stepped in and saved them from penury—who had cared enough about them to *want* to do that.

She could feel Vidal watching her, but she wasn't going to give him the satisfaction of looking back at him so that he could show her the contempt he felt for her.

'Are there any questions you wish to ask now about your late father's bequest to you before we continue?' the lawyer invited.

Fliss took a deep steadying breath. Here it was—the opportunity she so desperately wanted to ask the question that she so much wanted answering.

'There is something.' She had turned her body slightly in her chair, so that she was facing the lawyer and not Vidal, but she was still conscious of the fact that Vidal was focusing on her. 'I know that there was a family arrangement that my father would marry a girl who had been picked out for him as his future wife by his grandmother, but according to the letter you sent me he never married.'

'That is correct,' Señor Gonzales agreed.

'What happened? Why didn't he marry her?'

'Señor Gonzales is unable to provide you with the answer to that question.'

The harsh, incisive slice of Vidal's voice lacerated the small silence that had followed her question, causing Fliss to turn round and look at him.

'However, I can. Your father did not marry Isabella y Fontera because her family withdrew from the match. Though they made some other excuse, it was likely they got wind of the scandal surrounding him. His health had deteriorated, too, so no more matchmaking attempts were made. What were you hoping to hear? That he withdrew from it out of guilt and regret? I'm sorry to disappoint you. Felipe was not the sort of man to go against our grandmother.'

Fliss could feel her nails biting into her palms

as she made small angry fists of rejection. The golden gaze pinned her own and held it, making it impossible for her to escape from Vidal's thorough scrutiny of her. The way he was looking at her made her feel as though he would take possession of her mind and control her very thoughts if she let him. But of course there was no way she was going to do that. Pity indeed the woman he eventually married—because she would be expected to surrender the whole of herself, mind and body, to his control.

Her heart jolted against her ribs. In absolute contempt for what he was, Fliss assured herself, and certainly not because any foolish part of her was tempted to wonder what it would be like to be possessed so completely by a man like Vidal.

'What happened in the past happened, and I'd suggest that you would be a lot happier if you allowed yourself to move on from it.'

Fliss dragged her thoughts back from the dangerous sensuality they had escaped to and made herself focus on the sharp timbre of Vidal's voice.

'If you questioned your mother as antagonistically as you have spoken here you must have caused her a great deal of pain by never allowing the matter to be forgotten.'

The callousness of his accusation almost took Fliss's breath away. She had to fight not to let him see how easily he had found where she was most vulnerable, and defended herself immediately. 'My mother did not *want* to forget my father. She wore this locket he gave her until the day she died. She never stopped loving him.'

The gold locket chain shimmered with the agitated movement of the pulse beating at the base of Fliss's throat. Vidal could remember how it had shimmered with an equal but very different intensity of emotion the day Felipe had fastened it around Fliss's mother's neck.

It had been here in Granada that Felipe had bought the necklace for her. He had found them when they were on their way to visit the

Alhambra, announcing that some unexpected business had brought him there from the family estate. They had been walking past a jeweller's shop when he had caught up with them, and when Vidal had told Felipe that it was Annabel's birthday his uncle had insisted on going into the shop and buying the trinket for her.

Vidal shook his head, dragging his thoughts back to the present.

'The house is mine to do with as I wish, as I understand it,' Fliss said, and dared Vidal to contradict her.

'That is true,' the lawyer intervened. 'But since the house was originally part of the ducal estate it makes sense for Vidal to buy it from you. After all, you can have no wish for the responsibility of such a property.'

'You want to buy the house from me?' she challenged Vidal, her gaze steady.

'Yes. Surely you must have expected that I would? As Señor Gonzales has just said, the house belonged originally to the estate. If you are concerned that I might try to cheat you out of its true value—and I am sure that you are, given your obvious hostility towards me—I can assure you that I am not, and that it will be independently and professionally valued.'

Turning her back on Vidal, Fliss told the lawyer quickly, 'I want to see the house before it is sold.' When he began to frown she said fiercely, 'My father lived there. It was his home. Surely it's only natural that I should want to go there and see it, so I can see where and how he lived?'

The lawyer seemed uncomfortable, looking past her towards Vidal, as though seeking his approval.

'The house belongs to *me*,' she reminded him. 'And if I want to go there no one can stop me.'

There was a small silence, and then Fliss heard Vidal exhale.

'I have some business to attend to at the *castillo*, Luis,' he told the lawyer, using his Christian name for the first time. 'I will escort Felicity there tomorrow, so that she can satisfy her curiosity.'

The lawyer was looking relieved and grateful, Fliss recognised, as Vidal stood up, signalling that their meeting was over and saying, 'We shall meet again in a few days' time to progress this matter.'

Fliss noted that the lawyer avoided meeting her gaze when he shook hands with her before going, and that he and Vidal left the library together, leaving her still inside it and alone.

Alone.

She *was* alone now. Completely alone, with no family of her own. No one to support her; no one to protect her.

To *protect* her? From what? From Vidal? Or from those feelings Vidal aroused in her that led her body into responses to his maleness that were shamefully treacherous given what she already knew about him?

Shakily Fliss pushed the unwanted question away. So she had let down her guard accidentally, and somehow that had caused her to become aware of Vidal as a man. It had been a mistake, that was all—something she could put right by making sure that it didn't happen again.

The copy of her father's will that Señor Gonzales had given her was still on the desk. Fliss picked it up, her attention drawn to her father's signature. How many times as a child she had whispered that name over and over again to herself, as though it was some kind of magic charm that would cause her father to become a part of her life. But her father had *not* been part of her life, and she would not find him in the house in which he had lived. How could she when he was dead? She had to go there, though. She had to see it.

Because Vidal did not want her to?

No! Not because of that. Because of her father—not because of Vidal.

Fliss felt as though her emotions were threatening to suffocate her. She could hardly breathe from the force of her own feelings. She had to get out of this house. She had to breathe some air that was not tainted by Vidal's presence.

The hallway was empty when she walked through it, heading for the stairs and intent on getting her handbag and her sunglasses. She would go out and see something of the city—cleanse her mind of the unwanted influence that Vidal seemed to be exerting over it.

Ten minutes later Vidal watched from the library window as Fliss left the house. If he had had his way her departure would have been for the airport and England—and permanent. He had enough to think about without having her around, reminding him of things he would preferred to have left shrouded in the shadows of the past.

He still hadn't come to terms with his own behaviour last night—or with his inability to impose his will on his body.

CHAPTER FOUR

SHE had spent virtually all day exploring the city. The city, but not the Alhambra—she wasn't ready for that yet. She felt too raw after this morning's run-in with Vidal—too vulnerable to visit the place where her father had first declared his love for her mother, where the boy had witnessed that exchange and then reported it to his grandmother.

A small tapas bar had provided her with lunch. She hadn't been very hungry, and in fact felt she had not done proper justice to the delicious delicacies that had been served up for her.

Now, with her exploration of the conservation site that was the old Moorish quarter of the city behind her, she was forced to admit that her body had probably had a surfeit of hard pavements and intense sunshine. It craved the cool shade promised by the courtyard garden her bedroom overlooked.

The same shy maid who had brought her breakfast opened the door for her when she pulled the bell. Thankfully there was no sign of Vidal, and the library door remained firmly closed. She asked the maid how best she could get into the courtyard, thanking her when she explained that a corridor accessed from the rear of the hallway had a set of doors that opened into it.

While she was out she'd taken the opportunity to go shopping and buy some clothes to supplement those she had brought with her. Now that she was staying with the Salvetore family, rather than the hotel she'd booked, she realised she would need some more. After trying on a variety of things she had settled on a loosely gathered cotton dress in her favourite shade of cream, because it felt so light and cool, adding a simple linen shift in pale blue, a pair of tan cut-offs and a couple of softly shaped tops—cool, practical, easy-to-wear clothes in which she would feel much more comfortable than jeans and her city skirt.

In her bedroom, after a quick shower, she put on the cream dress. Simply styled, it was tiered in pleats from a square neckline banded with crunchy cotton lace. Worn with the flip-flops she had brought with her, the dress felt pleasantly cool and airy.

Back downstairs, she quickly found the corridor the maid had described to her, and the doors from it that led into the cloistered walkway that she could now see ran the full width of the courtyard. As she came out of the darkness of the corridor into the brightness of the sunlight beyond, momentarily dazzled by the light, Fliss came to an abrupt and self-conscious halt. She realised that she hadn't got the courtyard to herself.

The woman she could see seated at an ornate wrought-iron table, drinking a cup of coffee, had to be Vidal's mother. They had the same eyes—although in Vidal's mother's case their gaze was warm and gentle rather than cold and filled with contempt.

'You are Annabel's daughter, of course,' the Duchess said, before Fliss could retreat, adding, 'You are very like her. But I think you have something of your father's blood as well. I can see it in your expression. Please—come and sit here beside me,' she invited, patting the empty chair next to her own.

Hesitantly Fliss made her way towards her.

Tall and slender, her dark hair streaked with grey and worn in the kind of elegant, formal style that suited Spanish women so well, Vidal's mother smiled at her and apologised. 'I'm sorry I wasn't able to be here to welcome you yesterday. Vidal will have explained that I have a dear friend who is not very well.'

A small shadow darkened her eyes, causing Fliss to enquire politely, 'I hope your friend is feeling better?'

'She is very brave. She has Parkinson's disease,

but she makes light of it. We were at school together and have known one another all our lives.
Vidal tells me that he is taking you tomorrow
to see your father's house? I would have liked
to go with you, but my friend's husband was
called away unexpectedly on urgent business
and I have promised to keep her company until
he returns.'

'It's all right. I mean, I understand...' Fliss
told her truthfully. She stopped talking when
she realised that the Duchess was looking past
her into the shadows of the house, her smile
deepening as she exclaimed, 'Ah, Vidal, there
you are! I was just saying to Fliss how sorry I
am that I shan't be able to accompany you to the
castillo.'

Vidal.

Why was that quiver of sensation racing down
her spine? Why did she suddenly feel so aware of
her own body and its reactions, its womanhood
and its sensuality? She must stop reacting like

this. She must ignore these unwanted feelings instead of focusing on them.

'I'm sure Felicity understands why, Mamá. How is Cecilia?'

Immediately she registered Vidal's voice. Fliss's heart went into a flurry of small frantic beats that made her feel more breathless than she liked. It was because she hated him so much, she assured herself. Because she hated him for betraying her mother.

'She is very weak and tired.' The Duchess was answering Vidal, then suggesting to him, 'Why don't you join us for a few minutes? I'll ring for a fresh pot of coffee. Fliss looks very like her mother in her pretty cool dress, don't you think?' she asked.

'I suspect that Felicity has a very different personality from her mother.'

'Yes, I have—and I'm glad. My mother's gentleness meant that she was treated very unkindly.'

Fliss saw the colour leave the Duchess's face

and Vidal's mouth tighten. Her remark was not the kind a guest should make to her hostess, but she had not *asked* to stay here with her late father's family, Fliss defended herself, before turning on her heel and heading for the opposite end of the courtyard, wanting to put as much distance as she could between herself and Vidal.

The only reason she had chosen to escape further into the garden and not the house was that to get into the house she would have had to walk past him. Knowing how shamefully vulnerable her body was to him, that was something she had not been prepared to do. Now, hidden from view of the cloistered terrace by the shadows thrown by the rose-covered pergola at the bottom of the garden, Fliss lifted her hand to her heart to calm its angrily unsteady thudding.

The petals on the roses trembled as her sanctuary was penetrated. A tanned male hand brushed aside the branches, and pink petals swirled down onto the tiled pathway as Vidal stepped into the rose-cented bower formed by the pergola.

Without any preamble Vidal launched into his verbal attack, telling her coldly, 'You may be as antagonistic as you wish to me, but I will not have you hurting or upsetting my mother— especially at this time, when she has her friend's health on her mind. My mother has shown you nothing but courtesy.'

'That's true,' Fliss was forced to agree. 'However you're hardly the person to tell me how to behave, are you? After all, you obviously didn't have any qualms about intercepting my letter to my father, did you?' she accused him vehemently, her voice wobbling slightly over the final word.

Fliss was shaking inwardly and outwardly. Her one desire was to escape from Vidal's coldly critical presence before she made a complete fool of herself by telling him how unfairly he had misjudged her and how much that misjudgement had hurt her. How much it still hurt her.

Avoiding looking at him, she started to walk quickly back down the pergola—until she was brought to an abrupt halt when she slipped on the petal-scattered path.

The sensation of strong hands reaching for her, strong arms supporting her, brought her an initial and automatic surge of gratitude—but as soon as her body registered the fact that the hands and arms, like the body she was now being supported against, belonged to Vidal that gratitude was replaced by panic. Frantically Fliss struggled to free herself, thoroughly alarmed by the way her body was already reacting to the intimate contact between them.

For his part Vidal had no wish to hold on to her. Turning to watch her rush away from him, he had seen how the sunlight shining through her thin cotton dress revealed the female curves of her body, and immediately—to his grim disbelief—his body had responded to that sight and to *her*. Now, having her twisting and turning in his arms, her breasts rising and falling with agitation, her breath touching his skin in a silken caress, the scent and the feel of her was calling to an instinct within him that wouldn't be denied. An instinct that demanded he taste the erotically tender pink flesh of her lips, that he find and possess the soft rounded curves of her breasts, that he hold the cradle of her lower body close to the now swollen sexuality of his own.

In an attempt to push Vidal off, Fliss reached out wildly with her hand. Her whole body selate f with shock when her fingertips encountered the satin warmth of his bare chest. Fliss looked down at where her hand was resting and saw that Vidal's shirt was now unfastened almost to the belt of his chinos. Had *she* done that? Had she ripped open those buttons when she had clung to him earlier and then struggled against his confining grip? Her hand was now resting palm flat on his golden skin, and the dark cross of fine hair that narrowed downwards over his impressive six-pack made Fliss feel as though nature herself had used that male body hair to mark him out as her own.

Was it the scent of the roses or the scent of Vidal's skin that was making her feel so weak? She was forced to sway closer to him, her body bending pliably and willingly to his without needing to be guided there by the pressure of his hand on the small of her back, heating her body through the fine fabric of her dress. The topaz gaze was fixed on her own. Then as she caught her breath it slid deliberately to her mouth, capturing the small frantic moan of longing assent that escaped from her lips.

The quiver that shook her body as though she found her desire for him beyond her ability to control, that soft sigh of acquiescence, that liquid look of longing she had given him—they might all be a deliberate ploy to entice him, Vidal told himself. But whilst his mind might deride his folly for responding to them his body had no such inhibitions. Anger against it and against the woman he was holding exploded through him in a savage burst of primeval male need.

Beneath the fierce onslaught of his kiss Fliss's

already shaky defences gave way, her trembling lips opening to the demanding thrust of his tongue, her breast swelling into the cup of his hand. A heavy, aching sensation was rolling though her lower body and beginning an insistent pulsing beat that grew in tandem with the fiery burst of pleasure Vidal's probing fingers and thumb drew from the aroused tip of her breast.

Fliss had never thought of herself as a woman whose sensuality had the power to overwhelm her self-control. On the contrary, she had believed in her most private thoughts that she had an unfashionably low sex drive. But now, shockingly, Vidal was proving to her that that judgement of herself must have been wildly wrong. Her out-of-control and unwanted arousal, her need for the intimacy it was causing her to ache and long for, was sweeping through her like a forest fire, burning away any resistance that tried to stand in its way. Her desire to have Vidal touching the flesh of her breast had flamed into life well before Vidal had lifted its sensually engorged roundness free of her bra, so that her nipple was pushing eagerly against the tightly drawn fabric of her dress, its shape and even its dark rose colour easily visible beneath the thin fabric.

The sight of that enticement, that incitement to his own desire, had Vidal bending Fliss back in his arms and then lowering his head over her body, so that he could taste her nipple, so close in colour to the petals of the roses that were providing them with their privacy. Unable to stop herself, Fliss gave a soft, aching gasp of delirious pleasure. The sensation of his tongue stroking and caressing her so-sensitive flesh, one second soothing its need, the next tormenting with a flick of his tongue, was driving her to fresh heights of aching longing, and it stole away what was left of her self-control. Her spine arched, lifting her breast closer to Vidal's mouth.

The sheer wanton sensuality of the seeking movement of Fliss's body combined with the erotic feel of her hot, tight nipple against his tongue made Vidal forget what she was and where they were. At last—at last he had her in his arms, this woman whose memory so tormented him. His hold on her tightened as he drew her nipple deeper and harder into his mouth. Far from satisfying the volcanic ache of male need, that action only increased the savage torrent of desire rushing through him.

Bent back over Vidal's arm, clinging to his shoulders for support, Fliss could only shudder violently with previously unknown pleasure. A pleasure that was so intense it was almost more than she could bear. She wanted to tear her dress from her body and hold Vidal's mouth captive over her breast whilst he satisfied the growing tumultuous ache the fierce suckling movement of his mouth was creating—and at the same time she wanted to hide herself from him and what he was making her feel as fast as she could.

A cord of sensation like forked lightning zig-zagged inside her, running from her breast to the heart of her sexuality, making her want to plant her hand over that part of herself to both hide and calm its frantic hungry beat.

Scooping her up, Vidal pulled her tightly against him, so that she could feel his arousal, igniting another shaft of lightning within her as she responded to the sensual male message from his body.

Above her she could see the blue sky. She could smell the hot scent of their bodies mingling with the heady perfume of the roses. If he were to lay her down now and cover her flesh with his own—if he were to take her and possess her... Fliss felt her heart lift inside her chest and thud like a trapped bird. Wasn't this what she had wanted all those years ago when she had looked at Vidal and yearned for him?

Shock coursed through her, filling her with revulsion for her own behaviour, making her demand emotionally, 'Stop it—stop it! I don't want this.'

The frantic panic in her voice cut through

Vidal's own arousal, filling him with an appalled sense of self-disgust. What on earth had possessed him? He knew what she was. He had seen and heard it for himself.

As soon as he had released her Vidal turned his back to her, sharply aware of his body's hard arousal—an unwanted and unwarranted arousal as far as he was concerned. How could he have let that happen?

Shaking, Fliss adjusted her clothing, the pink stain colouring her face and her chest not just caused by her embarrassment. Her nipples ached painfully—not only the one Vidal had been caressing but the other one as well. Even something as simple and as necessary as breathing was bringing an uncomfortable awareness of their heightened sensitivity. Her sex itself felt hot and swollen, pressing against the barrier of her briefs, its dampness shamefully evident to her. She couldn't understand what had happened to her—how she could have gone from bitter anger to intense desire in the space of a handful of seconds just because Vidal had touched her. How *could* she feel like this?

Fliss focused on Vidal's disappearing back as he returned to the house. She wasn't going to allow herself to trail in his wake, following him like an adoring puppy, like the girl she had been at sixteen. And besides, the reality was that she didn't feel up to facing anyone else at the moment. Right now she preferred the privacy of the rose-covered arbour and its wrought-iron bench, where she could sit down and recover her composure.

It was a good ten minutes before she felt able to start walking back to the house. Ten minutes was surely long enough to ensure that Vidal was nowhere in sight, even if it hadn't been long enough for her heart to entirely resume its regular heartbeat. She was beginning to feel very afraid that that was never going to happen, and that she would be cursed for ever to bear the scars of the pain he had caused her.

Engrossed in her own thoughts, Fliss had all

but forgotten Vidal's mother until she reached the patio area and saw that the Duchess was still seated there. It was too late for her to retreat. The Duchess had seen her and was smiling at her, and besides...

Taking a deep breath, Fliss bravely stepped up to her, apologising with genuine remorse. 'I'm sorry if my comments upset or offended you. That wasn't my intention.'

An elegant long-fingered hand—a feminine version of her son's, surely?—clasped Fliss's arm gently.

'I suspect that I am the one who owes you an apology, Felicity. My son tends to be rather more protective of me than is always necessary. It comes in part because of the man he is, and from being head of such a traditional family, but also I think it comes because he was thrust into the role of head of the family at too young an age.' A shadow of remembered sadness touched her expression as she explained, 'My husband died when Vidal was seven.'

Fliss caught her breath in shock, unable to stop herself from creating inside her head an image of a seven-year-old boy learning that he had lost his father. Sympathy for Vidal? She must not weaken herself by going down *that* route!

'Then when Vidal was sixteen his grand-mother died—which meant that he had to take on the responsibilities of his inheritance.' She paused to say quietly, 'I'm sorry. I'm boring you, I expect.'

Fliss shook her head. She might be trying to tell herself that she wasn't interested in hear-ing Vidal's loving mother's stories of her son's youth, but the truth was that in reality a part of her wanted her to beg the Duchess to tell her more. It was disturbingly easy for her to picture Vidal at sixteen—tall, dark-haired, still a boy, but already showing the physical signs of the man he would become.

A small charge of sensation touched her skin; Vidal's touch, like Vidal's mouth against her flesh, had burned away barriers she had thought set in concrete—values and judgements.

Somehow she managed to drag her attention back to Vidal's mother, who was still speaking, telling her gently, 'Vidal was very attached to your mother, you know. He thought a great deal of her.'

Fliss managed to nod her head, although she couldn't trust herself to say anything.

Her mother hadn't really talked much about Vidal's mother—other than to say that she hadn't been Vidal's grandmother's first choice of a bride for her son, and that it was the Duchess who had insisted on Vidal having a more rounded and diverse upbringing than his paternal grandmother had wanted.

Unwittingly confirming what Fliss's mother had told her, the Duchess continued, 'My mother-in-law did not approve one little bit when I persuaded my late husband to hire a young woman to help Vidal improve his English. She thought it very unsuitable, and would have preferred a male tutor, but I felt that my little boy already had enough male influence over his life.'

Such a fond and loving warmth infused the Duchess's face that Fliss knew she was mentally picturing the child that Vidal had been. Fliss could picture that child too. Her mother had taken a good many photographs whilst she had been in Spain, and Fliss had grown up knowing who the dark-haired boy featured in some of them was. She had one of them with her now, in her handbag, taken at the Alhambra. It showed her mother and her father with a much younger Vidal, smiling into the camera through a curtain of water from a fountain. In it her mother had her arm round Vidal's shoulders—a protective, caring arm, as though, young as she herself had been, she was very aware of her responsibility towards the boy she was holding.

'Vidal's grandmother was a very strict disciplinarian who did not approve of what she thought of as my indulgence of Vidal.' The Duchess paused. 'Your mother suffered greatly at the hands of our family. Poor Felipe was such a quiet, gentle person. He hated upsets of any kind, and was very much in thrall to his adoptive grandmother. Understandably so. She had brought him up, following the death of his mother, according to her own strict regime and what she thought his mother would have wanted for him. He hadn't inherited any money from his parents and so was financially dependent on my mother-in-law. Felipe pleaded with her to be allowed to do the honourable thing and marry your mother, but she flatly refused to allow it. She wouldn't even agree to advance enough money to him to enable him to make financial provision for the two of you. She could be very unforgiving. In her eyes both Felipe and your mother had broken the rules, and deserved to be punished for doing so. Felipe had no money of his own, no home to offer your mother, no means of earning a living. His job within the family was that of managing the family orchards.'

'And his grandmother wanted him to marry someone else,' Fliss pointed out.

'She did,' the Duchess agreed. 'My mother-in-law could be very harsh at times—cruelly harsh, I'm afraid. I confess that I could never warm to her, nor her to me. But Vidal's father, like Vidal himself, was a very strong and moral man. He was in South America on business when his mother found out about the relationship. It is my belief that had he been here he would have done his best to see to it that matters were handled differently. As it was, he never returned. His plane crashed and everyone on board was killed.'

Fliss drew in a sharp breath, unable to stop herself from sympathizing. 'How dreadful.'

'Yes, it was, for all of us, but especially for Vidal. He had to grow up very quickly after that.'

Quickly, and into a man who was as harsh and unforgiving as the grandmother who had no doubt taken a hand in his upbringing, Fliss thought bitterly.

It was hard for a child to grow up with the death of one of its parents, but even harder for one parent to be alive and a child be denied contact. She could remember her mother answering her own naive childhood questions as to why her parents were not together and married.

'Your father's family would never have allowed us to marry, Fliss. Someone like me could never be good enough for him. You see, darling, men like your father, from important aristocratic families, have to marry girls of their own sort.'

'You mean like princes marrying princesses?' Fliss remembered asking.

'Exactly like that,' her mother had agreed.

'I had no idea that things had gone as far as they had when Annabel was sent away,' the Duchess was saying now, looking rather grim.

'I was conceived by accident on the night she and Felipe parted. Neither of them had intended... My mother said my father had always behaved like a perfect gentlemen, but the news that she was being sent away led things to get out of control.' Fliss immediately defended her mother, feeling that she was being criticised. 'My mother didn't even realise at first that she was pregnant. Then when she did her parents insisted that she write to my father to tell him.'

She wasn't going to have the Duchess thinking badly of her mother, who had, after all, been an innocent and naive young girl of eighteen, desperately in love and heartbroken at the thought of being parted from the man she loved.

'That was when my mother received a letter back saying that she had no proof that I was Felipe's child, and that legal action would be taken against her if she ever tried to contact Felipe again.'

The Duchess sighed and shook her head. 'My mother-in-law insisted. In her eyes, even if your mother had previously been acceptable to her as a wife for Felipe, the fact that she had allowed him such intimacies…' The Duchess gave a small shrug 'In families such as ours there is something of the long-ago traditions of the Moors with regard to the women of the family and the sanctity of their purity. In Vidal's grandmother's day girls of good family never so much as left the family home without the escort of a *duenna* to guard their modesty. That is all changed now, but I'm afraid a little of what has been passed down in the blood lingers. There is a certain convention, a certain fastidiousness, a certain requirement within the family that its female members abide by a moral code and that—'

'That brides are virgins?' Fliss suggested.

The Duchess looked at her. 'I would put it more that the men of the family are very protective of the virtue of their women. It has always been my belief that had Vidal's father returned safely to us here in Granada he would have insisted that your mother's innocence was honoured and your position within our family recognised. You are, after all, a member of this family, Felicity.'

The sight of the young maid coming out to ask if they wanted fresh coffee had Fliss shaking her head and excusing herself. It had been a long day. And tomorrow would be an even longer one now that she had insisted she wanted to see the house that had been her father's home, which he had now left her. A day in which she would be spending time in the company of the one man her instinct for self-preservation told her she should be spending as little time with as possible…

CHAPTER FIVE

'FELICITY, I KNOW that Vidal plans to leave immediately after breakfast tomorrow morning for the estate, so I won't keep you up any longer.'

The Duchess and Fliss were drinking their after-dinner coffee, sitting at a table on the vine-covered veranda outside the dining room.

Fliss had been very relieved indeed to discover that Vidal would not be joining them for dinner, as he already had an engagement with some friends.

It was true that she was feeling tired—drained, in fact, by the tension of the day—so she thanked the Duchess for her kind consideration and stood up, agreeing that she *was* ready for bed.

Having suspected that even though there would only be the two of them for dinner the Duchess would dress formally, Fliss was wearing her black dress, thankful that she had packed it. The jersey dress was an old favourite, and it looked good on her, she knew. She had bought it in a sale, and even then had baulked a little at the price, but the matt black fabric was cleverly cut and draped, and Fliss had quietened her conscience by saying that the dress was an investment piece that would earn its keep in terms of cost per wear.

She had washed and dried her hair before dinner, noticing that the sun had already lightened some of its strands.

It was not quite midnight—early, she knew, for the Spanish—but she had to smother a yawn as she made her way back to the main hallway and the stairs, through a succession of rooms all with imposing double doors that opened one into the other in the classical fashion, each one of them filled with heavy and no doubt extremely valuable antiques.

Upstairs in her bedroom Fliss noticed

appreciatively that the bed had been turned down invitingly for her, and that it had been made up with fresh sheets at some stage. It would be pure luxury to sleep in such beautiful sheets—Egyptian cotton, with an obviously high thread count, and smelling ever so faintly of lavender.

Her mother had always loved good-quality bedlinen. Had she developed that appreciation of it whilst she was in Spain?

Fliss sighed as she removed her dress.

Tomorrow she would see her father's house—his home—the home he had left to her, finally acknowledging her. Under the safe privacy of the shower she let her eyes fill with emotional tears. She would have willingly traded a hundred houses for a few precious weeks with her father and really getting to know him, she admitted stepping out of the shower and reaching for a towel, drying her damp body.

Wrapping a fresh towel round herself, she went into the bedroom to remove her sleep shorts and top from the drawer where she had placed them, hesitating when she looked towards the bed and imagined the cool smoothness of the luxurious sheets against her bare skin. Such a sensual pleasure—a small, private self-indulgence...

Smiling to herself, Fliss removed the towel and slid between the waiting sheets, breathing in blissfully as she did so. Their touch against her skin was even more heavenly than she had imagined, subtly easing the tension of the day from her body. She would sleep well tonight, and that sleep would equip her to face tomorrow— and Vidal.

Tiredly, Fliss switched off the bedroom lights.

In the silent garden below Fliss's closed bedroom windows, with only the stars to see him, Vidal frowned up at those windows. Right now, instead of standing here, dwelling with irritation on Fliss's behaviour and her insistence on seeing her father's house for herself, he should have been enjoying the charms of the elegant

Italian divorcée who had obviously been invited to his friends' dinner party as a dining partner for him. She had made her enjoyment of his company plain enough, discreetly suggesting that they conclude the evening *à deux* at her hotel. She'd been dark-haired, very attractive, and a good conversationalist. There would have been a time when he would have had no hesitation in accepting her offer, but tonight…

But tonight what? Why was he here, his mind filled with the irritation that Fliss was causing him, instead of in bed with Mariella? The reality was that, much as he'd enjoyed the company of his old friends, excellent though the meal had been, he had found his thoughts preoccupied with Fliss. Because of the problems she was causing him—that was why. There was no other reason. Was there?

His body was already reminding him of that unwanted ache of angry and unexpected desire she had aroused in it. He could still smell the scent of her body, still remember the taste of her. The taste and the feel.

Determinedly he suppressed the unwanted clamour of his senses. What he had felt was a momentary lapse, he assured himself, caused by his body's memory of a girl it had once desired. Nothing more than that. It was an aberration which was best ignored instead of focused on and thus allowed to grow beyond its real importance. It meant nothing. It was his problem and his misfortune—a misfortune that could never be revealed to anyone else—if he had come to realise there was a flaw in his nature that cleaved to an idealistic belief in a once-in-a-lifetime love, a flame that no other love could match.

In his case that flame had had to be extinguished.

Vidal knew himself. He knew that for him the woman he loved must be a woman he could trust absolutely to be loyal to their love in every single way. Felicity could never be that woman. Her own history had already proved that.

The woman he *loved*? Just because as a young man he had been foolish enough to look at a sixteen-year-old girl and create inside himself a private image of that girl as a woman it did not mean anything other than that he had been a fool. The innocence he had thought he had seen in Felicity—the innocence he had fought against his desire for her to protect—had been as non-existent as the woman created by his imagination. That was what he needed to remember—not the feelings she had aroused in him. There was no point in looking backwards to what might have been. The present and his future were what they were.

Grimly Vidal turned away from the window to walk back into the house.

'How long does it take to get to the *castillo*?'

Fliss's question was delivered through firmly controlled lips as she stared straight ahead through the windscreen of an imposingly luxurious limousine. She was seated in the passenger seat whilst Vidal pulled away from the family townhouse and into the busy morning traffic.

'About forty minutes—maybe fifty, depending on the traffic.'

Vidal's response was equally terse, his attention outwardly focused on the road ahead of him. Although inwardly he was far more aware of Fliss's presence in the car next to him than he liked to admit.

She was wearing a light-coloured summer dress, and as she had walked out to the car ahead of him he had seen how the sunlight striking through it revealed the long slender length of her legs and the curve of her breasts. Now, despite the leather smell of the car's upholstery, he could still smell the fresh scent of Fliss's skin—clean and yet subtly, erotically female—its delicacy causing within him an automatic need to move closer to her and so catch the scent properly.

Inside his head an image formed of Fliss's body pressed close to his in paganly sensual offering. Cursing inwardly, Vidal fought to suppress his own body's sexual reaction to that image, dropping his hand from the steering wheel and driving one-handed so that his arm could shield the physical evidence of his arousal from Fliss. He was thankful that she was staring ahead and not looking at him. The reality of seeing her now, as the woman she was and not the girl who had refused to leave his memory, should surely have diminished that desire—not increased it.

The silence between them was dangerous, Vidal acknowledged. It was allowing thoughts to flourish that he did not want to have. Better to silence them with mundane conversation than to give them free rein.

Keeping his voice neutral and distant, he told Fliss, 'In addition to showing you your father's house, I have some estate business to attend to before we return to Granada.'

Fliss nodded her head and then, unable to hold back the question, she asked him quickly, 'Did... did my mother ever visit my father's house?'

'Alone, you mean? To spend time in private with your father?'

Fliss could hear what sounded like disapproval in Vidal's voice. The same disapproval no doubt felt by his grandmother.

'They were in love,' she pointed out, immediately defensive of any criticism of her parents. 'It would only be natural if my father—'

'Had taken your mother to his house with the intention of bedding her, without any thought for her reputation?' Vidal shook his head. 'Felipe would never have done that. But then I suppose I shouldn't be surprised that *you* should think of it, given your own behaviour and sexual history.'

Fliss sucked in her breath, her lungs cramping tensely before she exhaled, furious shaky. 'You know nothing of the reality of either of those things.'

Vidal turned to look at her, disbelief hardening his expression. 'Are you seriously expecting me to listen to this? I know what I saw.'

'I was sixteen, and—'

'And a leopard doesn't change its spots.'

'No, it doesn't,' Fliss agreed furiously. 'You're the living proof of that.'

'Meaning what, exactly?' Vidal challenged.

'Meaning that I knew then what you thought of me, and why you judged me the way you did, and I know you still feel the same way now,' Fliss told him.

Vidal's hands tightened on the steering wheel. She had *known* how he had felt about her, despite all he had done to try and keep his feelings hidden from her—for her sake, not for his own? But of course she had, Vidal taunted himself. He had assessed her maturity and her readiness to know of his desire for her on her age, mistakenly believing her to be an innocent.

'Well, in that case,' he assured her curtly, 'no matter what you know, let me assure you that I do not intend to allow those feelings to affect my duty and my responsibility to carry out my late uncle's wishes with regard to your inheritance.'

'Good,' was the only response Fliss felt able to muster.

So it was true. She had been right. He had disliked her all those years ago and he still did now. She had already known that, so why did his confirmation of it make her feel so…so hurt and abandoned?

She had known how he felt about her when she came here. Or had she secretly been hoping for a miracle to happen? Had she been hoping for some kind of fairytale magic to wipe away the anguish she carried inside her? Leaving her free to… To what? To find a man with whom she could truly and completely be a woman, free to enjoy her sexuality without the stain of shame? Why did she need Vidal's belief in her innocence to do that? She knew the truth, after all, and that should be enough. Should be. But it wasn't, was it? There was something within her that could only be healed by… By what? By the touch of Vidal's hand against that sore place in reparation and acceptance of her as she really was?

It was her father she had come here to seek—not Vidal's acceptance of his misjudgement of her.

She had travelled a long way from the idealistic girl who had looked at Vidal and completely lost her heart. She knew that he was not the heroic figure she had created inside her head from her own adoration of him. He had shown her that himself when he had so misjudged her. There was no reason at all for her senses to be so aware of him now, for merely being here with him to make her ache with a dangerous resurgence of her teenage longing. But that was exactly what was happening.

Try as she might, she couldn't resist turning her head to look at him, imprinting his image on her senses.

The open neck of the shirt he was wearing revealed the straight line of his collarbone and the golden sleekness of his throat. If she looked properly at him no doubt she would be able to see where beneath his shirt his body hair lay.

She could remember the pattern of it from that time she had walked into the bathroom.

Stop it, Fliss exhorted herself desperately. The anxiety she was causing herself was raising tiny beads of sweat along her hairline, whilst her pulse and her heartbeat had started to thud nervously, as though in fear. She *was* afraid, she admitted. She was afraid of her own imagination and of the wilful power of the deep-rooted core of sensuality within her. It seemed to have grown out of nowhere, and previously she would have strenuously denied that she even possessed it.

Perhaps it was being here in her father's country that was unleashing previously hidden aspects of her make-up and bringing to life unfamiliar passions. It was much easier to cling to that thought than to allow herself to fear that it was Vidal himself who was responsible for this unwanted and dangerous flowering of such a deeply sensual side of her nature. Just as he had been when she was sixteen.

Vidal checked his rearview mirror—not

because he needed to do so, but because it would prevent him from glancing sideways at Fliss. Not that he needed to look at her to see her. Inside his head he had a perfectly visible image of her—although this image was one that, in defiance of his wishes, showed her eyes cloudy with arousal and her lips softly parted from his kiss. Such thoughts were not acceptable to him. And such desires…?

Grimly Vidal pressed his foot down on the car's accelerator. They were free of the city now, and the powerful car leapt forward.

As a pre-teenager, curious about her father and his homeland, but knowing that her mother found it painful to talk about him, Fliss had spent many hours in bookshops and the library, studying maps, descriptions and photographs of Granada and the Lecrin Valley. Later at university she had gone online to learn more, but no amount of that kind of exploration could come anywhere near the reality of the countryside they were now in.

She knew, of course, that the Lecrin Valley formed part of the natural Parque de Sierra Nevada, and that after the expulsion of the Moors from the area it had been left virtually untouched for many centuries, so that the countryside was dotted with a wealth of Moorish monuments, flour mills, and ancient castles in addition to the whitewashed Pablo villages that had once been home to the Moor population.

Orchards of orange and lemon trees, heavy now in the summer with ripening fruit, surrounded these small villages, with their narrow main streets and their small dusty squares, and the smell of the citrus fruit permeated the air inside the car despite its air-conditioning. Not that Fliss minded. In fact she loved the sharp, sun-warmed smell, and knew that it would be something she would carry with her once she had returned home.

'It must be so beautiful here in the spring, when the orchards are in blossom.' The words were out before she could stop them and remind herself that she had vowed this morning to remain as aloof from Vidal as she could.

'It is my mother's favourite time of year. She always spends the spring on our estate. The almond blossom is her favourite,' he responded, in a curt voice that showed Fliss how little he actually wanted to make any kind of contact with her at all, even though he had turned towards her as he spoke.

Pain flowered darkly inside her, like a bruise on wounded skin. Fliss's breath caught in her throat, in denial of what she was feeling, trapped there by the thudding sensation in her heart that merely looking at him brought her.

And she *was* looking at him, she recognised. Just like all those years ago in the bathroom, she was physically unable to remove her gaze from him. Why did this have to happen to her? Why could *this* man bring to life feelings within her that no other man had ever touched? Was there some part of her that wanted to be humiliated?

The flush burning her skin grew even hotter.

She mustn't think about Vidal. She must think instead about her parents, and about the love they had shared. She had been created out of that love, and according to her mother that made her a very special child. A child of love. Was it any wonder, knowing that, that she had been so stricken with shock and horror by Rory's behaviour that she had not been able to find the words to deny his lie about her? At sixteen she had naively believed that sexual intimacy should be a beautiful act of mutual love. She had had no desire whatsoever to experiment with sex, put off by what to her had seemed the coarse and vulgar attitude displayed by boys of her own age. Instead she had dreamed of a passionate, tender, adoring lover with whom she would share all the mysteries and delights of sexual intimacy.

And then Vidal had come to see her mother. The child she had heard so much about transformed into a hero who fitted her private template for what a man should be so perfectly that he had stolen her heart before she had even realised what was happening to her. Vidal—so handsome that just looking at him made her breath catch in her throat. Vidal—who carried about him such a powerful aura of male sensuality that even she at sixteen had been aware of it. Vidal—who knew her father. Was it any wonder that he had held so many of the keys that could unlock her emotional defences? Not that he had needed to unlock them. She had thrown down her barriers for him herself.

Shocked by her own vulnerability, Fliss tried determinedly to concentrate again on the countryside beyond the car window. They had turned off the main road now, and were travelling along a narrow road that was climbing between two outcrops of rock. Beyond them, she could see as the car crested the top of the incline, lay a lush, wide and fertile valley filled with orchards, and on the lower slopes of the ring of hills that enclosed it rows of vines.

'The boundary to the estate begins here,' Vidal told her, as they started to descend into the valley, still in that formal tone which told her how little he wanted her company and how much he wished she wasn't here with him.

Well, she didn't care. She wasn't here because of him, after all. She was here because of her father. But much as she tried to take comfort from that knowledge, comfort eluded her, and her aching heart refused to be soothed.

'You can't see the *castillo* yet, but it is at the far end of the valley—built there so that it could command a strategic position.'

Fliss caught a glimpse of the silver ribbon of a river, wending its way below them on the valley floor. The valley was a small perfect paradise, she recognised, caught off-guard by the unexpected sharp pang of envy that touched her as she thought of how wonderful it must have been to grow up here, surrounded by so much natural beauty. In the distance she could see the high peaks of the Sierras, and she knew that beyond the Lecrin Valley lay a sub-tropical coastline of great beauty.

But the coast and what lay beyond this place were forgotten as the road twisted and turned and then, up ahead of them, she could see the *castillo*. She had not realised it would be so large, so imposing, and her breath caught on a betraying gasp of awe. Its architecture was a blend of a traditional Moorish style and something of the Renaissance, and sunlight shone on the narrow iron-grille-covered windows of its turreted corners.

This wasn't a home, Fliss thought apprehensively. It was a fortress—a stronghold designed to reveal the might and the power of the man who held it and to warn others not to challenge that power.

They had to drive past formal gardens and an ornamental lake before reaching the front of the *castillo*, where Vidal brought the car to a halt.

An elderly manservant was waiting to greet them once they had stepped into the vast marble hallway, and a housekeeper who smiled far more warmly at her than Rosa was summoned to

escort her to her room after Vidal announced
that she might want an opportunity to 'freshen
up' whilst he spoke with his estate manager.

'Since it's almost lunchtime, I suggest that we
delay our visit to Felipe's house until after we
have eaten.'

Vidal might be using the word *suggest*, but
what he really meant, and wanted her to know,
was that he was giving her an order, Fliss thought
angrily, forced to nod her head and accept his
dictat, even though she wanted to insist that she
see her father's house immediately.

A couple of minutes later, following the housekeeper down a long, wide corridor on the second
floor, Fliss reflected that both the vastness of the
castillo and its architecture reminded her of a
long-ago visit to Blenheim, the enormous palace
given to the Duke of Marlborough by Queen
Anne. Here at the *castillo*, the ceiling of the long
gallery-style corridor was decorated with ornate
plasterwork, and the crimson-papered walls were
hung with huge gilt-framed portraits.

They had almost reached the end of the corridor when the housekeeper came to a halt and opened the double doors in front of her, indicating that Fliss was to precede her into the room beyond them.

If she had thought that her bedroom at the family townhouse in Granada was large and elegant, then she had obviously not realised what the words could actually mean, Fliss recognised. She put down the overnight bag she'd brought with her, lost for words in the middle of what had to be the most opulent bedroom she had ever seen.

Gilt swags and cherubs adorned the half-tester bed, whilst above it on the ceiling nymphs and shepherds rioted in discreet pastel-painted pastoral delight. Ornate gilt plasterwork decorated the cream-painted walls, framing insets of rich gold cherub-imprinted wallpaper, and matching silk curtains hung at the windows and fell from the bedhead.

All the furniture in the room was painted

cream—feminine and delicate—as well as
highly decorated with a good deal of gilt rococo
work. On the bed was a gold coverlet made out
of the same fabric as the curtains, its cherubs
stitched and padded to stand out. Against one
wall, between two sets of tall glass doors that
led out onto narrow balconies, stood a desk with
its own chair, and in the corner was a low table
on which she could see a selection of glossy
magazines. Fliss, who had a little knowledge
of antiques, suspected that the cream-and-gold
carpet was probably a priceless Savonnerie,
made especially for the room.

'Your bathroom and dressing room are through
here,' the housekeeper informed Fliss, indicating the recessed double doors on either side of
the bed. 'I shall send a maid up to escort you to
lunch in ten minutes.'

Thanking her, Fliss waited until the door had
closed behind her before investigating the bathroom and dressing room.

The bathroom was very traditional, with marble

floors and walls and a huge roll-top bath alongside a modern shower enclosure. Every kind of product a visiting guest might require was laid out on the marble surround to the basin. A quantity of thick fluffy towels hung from a modern chrome heated towel rail, whilst an equally thick and fluffy white robe hung from a peg behind the door.

The dressing room was lined with mirror-fronted cupboards large enough to hold the entire wardrobes of several families, and even possessed a *chaise-longue*. So that the male partner of the woman sleeping in the bedroom could lounge there and watch as she paraded in expensive designer clothes for his pleasure and approval? Inside her head Fliss had a swift mental image of Vidal, dark-browed and dark-suited, leaning against the gold silk upholstery of the *chaise*, reaching out to touch her bare shoulder, his gaze fixed on her mouth, whilst she—

No. She must not allow such thoughts.

Quickly stepping back into the bedroom, Fliss went over to open doors to one of the balconies, intending to breath in some fresh air. But she came to a halt when she saw that the balcony looked down on an enclosed swimming-pool area large enough to have belonged to a five-star hotel. The intense brilliant blue of the sky was reflected in the still waters of the pool, and beyond the walled pool area she could see the orchards, stretching up into the foothills.

This valley was a small earthly paradise—a paradise complete with its own danger, its own Lucifer as far as she was concerned, in the shape of Vidal. And was she tempted by Vidal as Eve had been tempted by the serpent, in danger of risking all that mattered to her morally for the sake of the sensual caress of a man who represented everything she most despised?

CHAPTER SIX

SOMEONE was knocking on her bedroom door. Quickly removing her rolled-up Panama hat from her case and grabbing her handbag, Fliss went to open the door, somehow managing to disengage herself from her troublesome thoughts and produce a smile for the maid who was waiting outside it.

In the room to which the maid showed her a buffet lunch had been laid out on a heavily carved wooden sideboard. Three places were set at the immaculately polished mahogany table, and the reason for that was made apparent when Vidal walked into the room, accompanied by a good-looking dark-haired younger man, who gave Fliss a warm smile of open male appreciation as soon as he saw her.

Vidal introduced them. 'Felicity—Ramón Carrera. Ramón is Estate Manager here.' Ramón's warm smile faded to a very respectful inclination of his head when Vidal added, 'Felicity is Felipe's daughter,' before striding over to the buffet and telling them both, 'Come—let us eat.'

Going to pick up one of the plates on the table, Fliss grappled with the unexpectedness of Vidal introducing her openly as his adopted uncle's daughter—thus acknowledging her as a member of the family as easily as though there had never been any past secrecy or unwillingness to recognise her. Why had he done it? Because he had felt it necessary to explain her presence and hadn't wanted anyone on the estate to jump to the conclusion that just because he had brought her here it meant they were personally involved romantically? Of course, being the man he was, he wouldn't want anyone thinking that. He had made his dislike of her plain enough, after all.

As she ate her food, whilst the two men talked

about estate matters, Fliss pondered on why the thought of Vidal pointing out that she was here because she was Felipe's daughter and *not* because of any personal emotional involvement with him had the power to make her feel such an intense stab of angry pain.

'You have not tried our wine yet,' she heard Ramón saying, 'It's a new Merlot we have just started producing here.'

Dutifully Fliss raised the glass of red wine to her lips and breathed in its heady bouquet, intrigued by the hint of what smelled like scented blossom mixed with the rich smell of the wine itself, before taking a cautious sip. She had been right to be cautious, Fliss recognised, as she felt the wine's full-bodied warmth spreading through her body.

'It's excellent,' she told Ramón truthfully,

'It is Vidal who deserves your praise, not me.' Ramón smiled. 'It was his idea to import some new vines from a vineyard in Chile in which he has a financial interest, to see if we

could replicate the excellent wine they produce
there.'

'What we have produced here is unique to
this area.' Vidal joined in the conversation.
'Something of the smell of our orchards has
been incorporated in the wine.'

'Yes, I noticed that,' Fliss agreed, taking another sip from her wine glass. The wine really
was good. Its scent was making her want to bury
her nose in the glass to breathe in more of it.

'Vidal said that he wanted to produce a Merlot
that reminded him of riding through the orchards
on a warm spring morning,' Ramón enthused.
'A lovers' wine that is full of promise and the
joy of being alive. It has been very well received
in the industry. I think, Vidal, that we should
perhaps have named it for Señor Felipe's oh-so-
beautiful daughter,' Ramón told Vidal, giving
Fliss another admiring look.

Vidal felt as though someone had sliced straight
into his gut as he watched Fliss smile warmly
at Ramón. She had not mentioned there being

a current man in her life, but even if there was, given what he knew about her, she was hardly likely to think it necessary to stop at one—especially when she was far away from him.

Abruptly he stood up, announcing brusquely, 'We should make a move, I think. You will report back to me about that problem with the irrigation system before tonight, please, Ramón. If we are going to have to get a senior engineer out I would prefer it to be tomorrow, whilst I am still here.'

'I'll go and find out what's happening,' Ramón confirmed, rising from his own chair and then coming to hold Fliss's chair for her with a courtly gesture as she too moved to stand up.

Excusing himself to go and get on with his work, Ramón left Fliss and Vidal to walk out into the early-afternoon sunshine together.

Since she had expected that her father's home would be within walking distance of the *castillo*, Fliss was surprised when Vidal placed his hand beneath her elbow to direct her back towards the car. She could feel first her arm and then her whole body burning with the heat caused by her proximity to him, causing her an immediate panic and a need to get away from him. It would be unbearable if he should guess the effect he had on her. Fliss could just imagine how much he would enjoy the humiliation that would bring her. But no amount of fear of that humiliation though was enough to stop her nipples from hardening to push determinedly against the covering of her bra and her dress. It was almost as though they wanted to shame her by flaunting their arousal and their willing availability in front of Vidal.

Angry with herself, she took refuge from her unwanted sensual vulnerability to him and her inability to control it by telling him scornfully, 'I suppose it's beyond your dignity as a duke to walk to the house?'

This drew a grim look from him as he told her coldly, 'Since it's a mile-and-a-half walk along the road, or a mile as the crow flies, I thought it would be easier to use the car. However, if you prefer to walk…' He looked down at Fliss's flimsy sandals as he spoke, causing her to recognise with a new surge of anger that he had won that particular run-in between them.

They had travelled quite a distance down the long drive, in a silence that bristled with mutual hostility, before Vidal announced in a peremptory tone that would have immediately got Fliss's back up even without the added insult of what he had to say, 'I must warn you against indulging in a flirtation with Ramón.'

'I was *not* flirting with him,' Fliss snapped in outrage.

'He made it plain that he found you attractive, and you allowed him to do so. Of course we both know how eager you are to accommodate the desires of any man who chooses to express them to you.'

'Trust you to throw that in my face.' Fliss tried to defend herself. 'You just couldn't wait to do so, could you? Well, for your information—'

'For *your* information,' Vidal interrupted her coldly, 'I will not have you indulging your promiscuous sexual appetite with Ramón.'

She must not let the pain of what he was saying touch her. If she did—if she let it into her heart—then it would surely destroy her. It proved how vulnerable she already was that she should actually feel herself aching to tell him that he was wrong, and demand that he listen to the truth. Vidal would never listen to the truth because he didn't want to hear it. He wanted to think the worst of her—just as he had wanted to prevent her from making contact with her father. To him she was someone who just wasn't good enough to be treated with compassion and understanding.

'You can't stop me taking a lover if I want to, Vidal.' It was the truth, after all.

Without looking at her, Vidal replied grimly, 'Ramón is married, with two young children. Unfortunately his marriage is going through a difficult time at the moment. Ramón is known to have an eye for pretty girls, and his wife is not at all happy about his behaviour. I have no wish to see their marriage fall apart and their children left without a father, and I promise you, Felicity, that I will do whatever it takes to make sure that does not happen.'

Vidal had turned off the main drive and onto a narrow, less well-maintained track, at the end of which, rising above the heavily laden orange and lemon trees, Fliss could see the top storey and attic windows of a red-roofed house. It gave her the perfect, much-needed excuse not to respond to Vidal's crushing comment, but instead to retreat into what she hoped was a dignified silence—whilst her heart thumped jerkily against her chest wall in a mixture of anger and chagrin.

In that silence Vidal drove them through what felt like a tunnel of spreading branches. Sunlight dappled through them to create an almost camouflage effect on the bark of the trees, and the crops in the close-mown grass below them. And then Fliss got her first proper glimpse of the house. Her breath caught in her throat, her heart flipping dizzily with emotion. If it was possible to fall in love with a house then she just had, she recognised.

Three storeys high, whitewashed, it filled her with delight. There was delicate detail in its iron-grille-surrounded balconies, and there were bright slashes of colour from the geraniums tumbling from pots outside the house and the bougainvillea blossom against the lower walls of the house. Oddly, there was something almost Queen Anne about the architectural style of the building, so that there was a familiarity about it—as though somehow it was welcoming her, Fliss thought emotionally as Vidal brought the car to a halt outside a pair of wooden double doors.

'It's beautiful.' The words were said before she could call them back.

'It was originally built for the captive mistress of one of my ancestors—an Englishwoman seized in a fight at sea between my ancestor's ship and an English vessel in the days when the countries were at war with one another.'

'It was a *prison*?' Fliss couldn't hold back her distaste.

''If you want to see if that way. But what I would say is that it was their love for one another that imprisoned them. My ancestor protected his mistress by housing her here away from the judgement of society, and she protected the heart he had given her by remaining true to him and accepting that his duty to his wife meant that they could never officially be together.'

After what Vidal had told her, Fliss had expected the house to wear an air of sadness and disillusionment, but instead the first impression she had when she stepped into the cool white-painted hallway with its tiled floor was that the house was holding itself still, as though in expectation of something—or someone. Her father?

The air smelled soft and warm, as though the house was regularly aired, but Fliss thought that beneath that scent she could still smell a hint of male cologne. An ache of unexpected longing and sadness swept through her, catching her off-guard, so that she had to blink away her betraying emotion. She had genuinely thought that she had wept all the tears she had to weep for the father she had never known many, many years ago.

'Did my…did my father live here alone?' she asked Vidal—more to break the silence between them than anything else.

'Apart from Ana, who was his housekeeper. She has now retired and gone to live in the village with her daughter. Come—I shall show you the house, and then once you have satisfied your curiosity I shall return you to the *castillo*.'

Fliss could sense that Vidal was holding both his impatience and his dislike of her on a very short rein.

'You didn't want me to come here, did you? Even though my father left the house to me?' she accused him.

'No, I didn't,' Vidal agreed. 'I didn't and don't see the point.'

'Just like you didn't see the point of me writing to him. In fact as far as you are concerned it would have been better if I had never been born, wouldn't it?'

Without waiting for Vidal's reply—what was the need, after all, when she already knew the answer to her own question?—Fliss moved further into the house.

Although it was far more simple in style and decoration than the *castillo*, it was still furnished with what Fliss suspected were valuable antiques.

'Which was my father's favourite room?' she demanded, after she had walked though a well-proportioned drawing room and explored the elegant, formal dining room on the opposite side of the hallway, as well as a smaller sitting room and a collection of passages, storerooms, and a small businesslike office situated at the back of the house.

For a minute she thought that Vidal wasn't going to answer her. His mouth had hardened, and he looked away from her as though impatient to be free of her company. She held her breath.

But then, just as she thought he was going to ignore her, he turned back to her and told her distantly, 'This one.' He opened the door into a small library. 'Felipe loved reading, and music. He…' Vidal paused, looking into the distance before he continued. 'He liked to spend his evenings in here, listening to music and reading his favourite books. The sun sets on this side of the house, and in the evening this room is particularly pleasant.'

The image Vidal was painting was one of a solitary, quiet man—a lonely man, perhaps—who had sat here in this room, contemplating what might have been if only things had been different.

'Did you…did you spend a lot of time with him?' Fliss could feel the words threatening to block her throat. Her hand went to it, tangling with the slender gold chain that had been her mother's, as though by touching it she could somehow ease away the pain she was now feeling.

'He was my uncle. He managed the family orchards.' Vidal gave a shrug which Fliss interpreted as dismissive and thus uncaring. 'Naturally we spent a good deal of time together.'

Vidal was turning away from her. Releasing her chain, Fliss looked back at the desk, her attention caught by the gleam of sunlight on the back of a small silver photograph frame. Driven by an impulse she couldn't control, she picked it up and turned it round. Her heart slammed into her ribs as she looked down at a photograph of her mother, holding a smiling baby Fliss knew to be herself.

Her hand shaking, she put the photograph down.

Vidal's mobile rang, and whilst he turned away to take the call Fliss studied the photograph again. Her mother looked so young. So proud of her baby. What had her father thought when he had seen the photograph? Had he been filled with regret—guilt—even perhaps longing to have the woman he loved and the child he had created with her there with him? She would never know now.

He had kept the photograph on his desk, which must mean that he had looked at it every day. Fliss tried to drive away the feeling of deep sadness permeating her, but still her questioning thoughts tormented her. Had he ever hoped that one day they would meet? He had never made any attempt to contact her.

Vidal had ended his call.

'We have to get back to the *castillo*,' he told her. 'Ramón has arranged for me to see the water engineer. A decision needs to be made with regard to the problem with our water supply. We can come back here in the morning if you wish to see upstairs.'

His voice suggested that he couldn't understand

why she should want to, but Fliss had a more pressing question she wanted to ask.

'Did my father know about my mother's death?'

She could see the way Vidal's chest lifted as he breathed in.

'Yes, he did know,' he told her.

'How do you know he knew?'

She didn't need to see the way Vidal's mouth compressed or to hear his irritably exhaled breath to know that she was testing his patience. But she didn't care.

'I know because I was the one who had to break the news to him.'

'And he...*no one* thought that I might have needed to hear from him, my only living relative, my father...?'

All the pain she had felt at losing her mother at eighteen came rushing back over her.

'It was you—you who kept us apart,' she accused Vidal.

The look in Vidal's eyes silenced her, choking the breath from her lungs.

'Your father's health suffered a great deal when he was parted from your mother. His doctor felt that it was best that he lived a quiet life, without any kind of emotional pressure. For that reason, in my judgement—'

'In *your* judgement? Who were *you* to make judgements and decisions that involved me?' Fliss demanded bitterly.

'I was and am the head of this family. It is my duty to do what I think right for that family.'

'And preventing me from seeing my father, from knowing him, was what you thought "right", was it?'

'My family is also your family. When I make decisions concerning it I make them with due regard to all those who are part of it. Now, if you can manage to cease indulging in this welter of infantile emotionalism, I would like to get back to the *castillo*.'

'To see the engineer—because watering your

crops is more important than considering the harm you have done and owning up to it.' Fliss gave a bitter laugh. 'Of course I should have realised that you are far too arrogant and cold-hearted to ever *think* of doing anything like that.'

Without waiting for him to reply, she headed for the door.

Fliss looked down at the food on her plate with a heavy heart, her hand going to her throat, where her mother's chain should have been. She could still feel the cold shaft of dismay she had felt when she had looked in her bedroom mirror and realised that it wasn't there.

At first she'd hoped that it had simply come loose and slipped down inside her top, but when several careful searches of the clothes she had removed and then the entire bedroom floor had not revealed the precious memento of her mother, she had been forced to recognise the truth. She had lost the chain and locket that had been such a treasured link not just with her mother but also her father—because he had given the jewellery to her mother in the first place.

Her distress went too deep for the relief of tears, and so, dry-eyed and heavy-hearted, she had forced herself to change for dinner into her black dress—just as she was—trying desperately to force herself make polite conversation with Ramón's wife, Bianca.

The estate manager and his wife had been invited to join them for dinner—as a way of underlining the warning Vidal had given her earlier with regard to Ramón himself? Fliss wondered a little grimly. If so, there had been no need. Even without his wife she would not have felt inclined to encourage Ramón's lunch-time would-be flirtation with her. Charming though the estate manager was, his presence did not provoke any kind of desirous feeling within her, never mind create those feelings to the self-control-obliterating extent that Vidal's presence did.

Fliss's fork clattered down onto her plate as she fought to deny what she had just admitted to herself. By what cruel trick of nature could it have happened that she was so intensely and physically aware of and responsive to the one man above all others she should have been safe from finding in any way attractive?

Picking up her fork, she turned her attention to Bianca in an attempt to distract herself. Ramón's wife was an attractive, if rather remote-looking woman in her early thirties, with classically Spanish good looks. Given what Vidal had told her about Ramón, it was perhaps not surprising that Bianca's manner towards her should betray some reticence Fliss acknowledged, and she herself was hardly in the right mood to set about reassuring the other woman and drawing her out—although the good manners her grandparents and mother had insisted upon were urging her to do her best.

There were several times, though, when she wasn't able to prevent her hand from creeping up to her throat in search of the missing chain, and a shadow clouded her eyes when she was forced to accept its absence.

A white wine from the vineyard in Chile in which Vidal had a financial interest was served with their meal of fish, caught locally on the coast, and then a sweeter wine was poured by Vidal when the dessert arrived—an almond dish made from the estate's own almonds.

It was when he was filling her glass that he said unexpectedly to Fliss, 'You aren't wearing your chain.'

The fact that he had noticed it in the first place was enough to catch Fliss off-guard, even without the emotional pain of having to acknowledge its loss, but somehow she managed to control her reaction and admit huskily, 'No. I seem to have lost it.'

Was she imagining the way in which Vidal's gaze lingered on her throat before he moved on to fill first Ramón's and then his own glass? Her vulnerable flesh was certainly burning as though it had.

Desperate not to either think about her lost chain and locket or her contradictory reactions to Vidal, Fliss focused her attention again on Bianca, asking her about her children. She was rewarded with the first genuine smile the other woman had given her all evening, and Bianca launched into a catalogue of the wonderfulness of their two young sons.

Listening to her, Fliss couldn't help wondering what it must feel like to have a child and be a mother—to feel that sense of joy and fierce maternal pride she could see so clearly in Bianca's response. Bianca had produced a photograph of their sons. Dark-haired and dark-eyed, with warm olive skin, they looked like miniature images of their father.

Against her will, Fliss's gaze was drawn to Vidal, who was now deep in conversation with Ramón about the engineer's recommendations for fixing the problem with the water. Of course, she had no need to try to imagine what Vidal's sons would look like. After all, she had a photograph of Vidal himself as a boy. She had grown up with that image and it was surely imprinted within her for ever. His sons' mother would contribute to their gene pool, too, though, and she would be…

She would be everything that she herself was not, Fliss reminded herself, her hand trembling as she held her wine glass. Why on earth should she care who Vidal married, what his sons would look like, or even if he had any? Why, indeed? And equally, why did she have that curious ache of mixed longing and loss deep inside her body, right where her womb was?

CHAPTER SEVEN

THE evening was over, and Fliss was back in her bedroom. The bareness of her neck against the snowy backdrop of the towelling robe she had pulled on after her shower reminded her of what she had lost and filled her with fresh guilt.

Her mother had always worn, treasured, and guarded her locket. Fliss didn't have a single visual childhood memory in which she could *not* see it round her mother's neck, and now *she* had lost it through her own carelessness. Somehow in its own way that hurt as deeply and painfully as the loss of her mother herself, and brought back for her the confused and unhappy feelings she had had as a young child, questioning why she did not have a father. That chain and its locket had bound her parents together, and through that bonding it had bound them to her as well. It had been her only material connection that was shared by them both, and now it was gone. That precious link had been broken.

But she still had another link with her father, Fliss reminded herself. She still had the house that he had left her.

Only for now, she reminded herself. Vidal had made it clear that he both expected and wanted her to sell it to him.

Fliss was just on the point of slipping out of the bathrobe and getting into bed when a knock on her door came. Hastily pulling the robe back onto her shoulders and clasping it closed in front of her, she went to answer the knock, assuming that it must be one of the maids.

Only it wasn't one of the maids. It was Vidal, and now he was inside the room and closing the door behind him.

'What do you want?' Would he hear the anxiety in her voice and guess that it came from an awareness of her own vulnerability to him?

Fliss hoped not as she watched his mouth twist in cynical contempt.

'Not *you*, if that is what you are hoping for. A man—any man to satisfy the desire you probably hoped to extinguish with Ramón? Is that what you hoped I might be, Felicity?'

'No!' The denial was torn from her throat.

Make-up-free, her hair tousled and her feet bare, not to mention the fact that her body was equally bare beneath the enveloping robe, Fliss was acutely conscious of feeling at a disadvantage compared with Vidal, who was naturally still wearing the light wool suit and the pale blue shirt he had worn during dinner.

But it was her emotional vulnerability to him that disadvantaged her more, she told herself as Vidal dismissed her denial with a savage, *'Liar. I know you, remember?'*

'No, you don't. You don't know me at all. And if you've come here just to insult me—'

'Is it possible to insult a woman like you? I should have thought you were beyond that—a woman who gives herself to all and sundry in a tawdry mockery of what man-to-woman intimacy should really be.'

The words he spoke, each insult he made, felt like a knife wound to her heart and her pride.

'I've brought you this,' Vidal told her curtly, changing the subject, and opening his hand to reveal her chain and locket nestling in his palm

The sight of it robbed Fliss of the ability to speak. She had to blink and look again to make sure that she wasn't seeing things.

'My locket,' she said, and she shook her head in disbelief as she switched her gaze to his face to demand disjointedly, 'How…? Where…?'

Vidal's shrug was dismissive, almost bored, Fliss felt, as he told her, 'I remembered that you were wearing it when we went into the house, so it seemed logical that you might have lost it there. After I had said goodnight to Bianca and Ramón, I drove over there. I recalled that you were playing with the chain when we were in

Felipe's office, so I started my search there, and as luck would have it that was where I found it—on the floor next to the desk.'

'You did that for…?'

For me, she had been about to say, but she was glad that she'd paused before doing so when he told her flatly, 'I know how much it meant to your mother and how she cherished it.'

Vidal made himself cut across the hesitant vulnerability he could hear in Fliss's voice. He didn't want to see her as vulnerable or deserving of compassion, because if he did—if he allowed that image of her into his head and his heart—it would mean… It would mean what?

It would mean *nothing*, Vidal assured himself grimly.

Fliss nodded. 'Yes. Yes, she did.' Of course he had not gone to look for it for *her.* Vidal would never do anything for her. 'I'm glad you found it,' was all she could allow herself to say, and she reached out to take it from him, her outstretched fingers curling back into her palm as she recoiled from actually touching him. Because she was afraid. Of what? Afraid of touching him, or afraid that once she did she wouldn't be able to stop?

He shouldn't have come here. He had known that. So why *had* he? Vidal derided himself. To test his self-control? To prove that he could walk through fire? To suffer the torment he was now suffering? He knew that beneath her robe Felicity was naked. He knew that given her sexual history, her sexual proclivities, he could reach for her and take her now, satiate himself in her, with her, until the need that gnawed unceasingly at him, that cried out to him, was silenced.

A tremor knifed through Fliss's body.

'Take it,' Vidal demanded, holding out his hand to her, the gold glistening in his palm.

For a moment they looked at one another, neither of them saying anything. Fliss's breathing and her balance were both slightly unsteady as her senses registered the sensual tension in the air between them. Vidal lifted his hand, and for a second Fliss thought that he was going to reach out and touch her. She moved back from him, forgetting that a low table was right behind her until she stepped back into it.

She heard Vidal curse as she stumbled, but even then she held up her hands to fend him off, prepared to fall rather than risk being touched by him. Only it was already too late. His hands were gripping her upper arms, and his face was hard with hostility and contempt as his gaze raked her face and then fell to the now open front of her robe.

One of them made a small sound. She wasn't sure if it was Vidal or herself. Her chest lifted abruptly, its movement driven by an urgent need to expand her lungs and take in more oxygen. Time seemed to hold its breath. She was certainly holding her own breath, Fliss knew, as they looked at one another in silence. Was she the first to break that eye contact, her gaze drawn helplessly down to Vidal's mouth, her own lips parting on a quivering gasp of longing? Fliss didn't know. She only knew that when she looked up into Vidal's eyes again they were smouldering with the sensual intent of a man who knew that the woman he was with wanted him.

'No.'

Her denial was a soft, agonised sound of despair, but Vidal ignored it. His gaze was obscured, so she couldn't see what was in his eyes as he looked down at her mouth. Fliss's heart was thundering with reckless, out-of-control thuds, driven by her heightened awareness of both him and her own longing. She watched as he lowered his head, his lips almost touching her own, his breath an unbearably tormenting caress against her mouth. Unable to stop watching, Fliss moved closer to him.

'Damn you!'

Fliss could hear the anger in Vidal's voice as he thrust her away from him. Her chain lay on the floor between them. Instinctively she moved forward to pick it up, and then froze in shock when Vidal took hold of her again.

'You just can't stop yourself, can you? *Any* man will do, won't he? Any man as long as he gives you this.'

He was kissing her, and she could feel his contempt. She could taste it. He wanted to humiliate her, to destroy her, and she wanted… She wanted to make him see that he was wrong about her. She wanted to punish him for misjudging her. She wanted to see his pride lying shredded in the wreckage of his misconceptions. And now she could do that. Now she could turn his anger-fuelled passion into her own salvation. The sacrifice of her belief that sexual intimacy should be something born out of mutual love would ultimately be Vidal's humiliation.

Maybe this had always been meant to happen? Maybe it was the only way she would ever be able to walk free of the emotional pain he had caused her? Maybe this was something she needed to experience to be able to finally destroy the foolish dreams she had once had?

Slowly and deliberately, as though her body

was weighted and drugged, Fliss moved closer to Vidal, deliberately grinding her lower body into his in a motion she had seen actors using. She lifted her hand to the buttons on Vidal's shirt, concentrating on unfastening them as his tongue thrust fiercely against her own. A quiver of sensation ran through her but she ignored it. This wasn't about her own desire—at least not her own desire for Vidal—it was about her desire to be free of everything in her life that had been tied to him.

His shirt was unfastened now, and he was still kissing her. A hard, demanding kiss without any softening warmth or tender emotion. How long would it be before his anger cooled and he pushed her away again? She must not let that happen. Somehow she must keep feeding his anger until it became physical arousal and desire. And perhaps the best way to do that was to confirm his judgement of her.

Very carefully and deliberately she broke Vidal's kiss, and then equally deliberately she let the robe slide from her body. She stepped towards him and placed her lips against his, lifting her hands to his shoulders.

She heard Vidal groan, felt his hands clamping down on her waist, his mouth closing against hers.

A shiver of self-revulsion gripped her. What was she doing? She had gambled and lost in a mad moment of self-destruction, and now…

He couldn't let this happen. Vidal knew that. He would be damned for ever if he gave in to Felicity's allure. And tormented for ever if he did not. His body yearned and ached for her. For seven years he had had to live with the need she aroused in him. He looked down at her body and felt his own shudder violently as he fought against taking what she was offering. Of its own volition and against his will his hands lifted from her waist to her breasts, full and taut, the nipples already hard with sensual promise. They pressed against his palms.

'Oh!' Fliss gasped, caught off-guard by the

shock of pleasure the sensation of Vidal's touch against her breasts had brought. She hadn't been expecting it and it widened her eyes and made her mouth soften. Desire? Her body trembled. Was it wrong to want him, or was it part of what must happen?

Vidal could see and feel Fliss's arousal. She wanted him! That knowledge severed the last strand of his self-control, plunging him into the millrace of his own longing for her.

He tried to dam the racing flood of his need. His heart was slamming into his chest wall. He knew what he should do, but it was impossible for him to stem the fierce tide of desire that possessed him. At some atavistic deep level his instinct said that Felicity was *his*—should always have been his, would be his.

Her lips clung to his, parting eagerly to the thrust of his tongue as he took and tasted the wild sweetness of her mouth.

Beneath the possessive pressure of Vidal's kiss, Fliss tensed on a soft moan of delight.

There was no point in her trying to control the desire leaping to life inside her, racing from nerve-ending to nerve-ending. Why attempt the impossible? Why resist what was surely preordained by fate?

The seeking, all-conquering exploration of his tongue took her own into its fierce possession, sending a starburst of liquid arousal spilling through her whole body. And when Vidal withdrew his tongue from hers, to stroke the tip of it tormentingly against the now swollen fullness of her lips, Fliss clung to him, cast adrift in a wild inner sea of sensual intensity.

The reason they were here together like this no longer mattered. It had evaporated like morning mist beneath the heat of the sun, burned away by the power of their shared desire.

Now it was Fliss who captured Vidal's tongue, taking it deep within the warm wet intimacy of her mouth to caress it with her own. She was in Vidal's arms, and they were kissing as though the connection between them had sprung to life like an invisible force that bound them together.

She welcomed the possession of Vidal's hands against her naked breasts, straining towards him as though to offer him their arousal, her whole body shuddering wildly when he rolled her nipples between his thumb and forefinger in a caress of erotic delight that had her digging her nails into the hard muscles of his arms.

Vidal didn't need her to tell him what he was doing to her, or what she wanted. He seemed to understand her need instinctively, arousing it, matching it, feeding and sustaining it with his touch and the growing passion of his kisses.

She had no will apart from the will to submit to the pleasure Vidal was giving her, Fliss thought dizzily, lost in the erotic heat that enveloped her, enclosing her in its embrace, possessing her senses, her thoughts and her will-power just as Vidal was possessing her body. She wanted what was happening more than she had ever wanted anything in the whole of her life. It was what she had been born for, what she longed for. It was her fate and her destiny—a completion that had the power to make her whole.

Vidal's hands moulded and caressed her breasts as he kissed her again, the rhythm of his fingers caressing the eager hardness of her nipples and matching the equally rhythmic thrust of his tongue against her own, creating a swiftly growing crescendo of hungry longing that pulsed and ran through her body in a silent song of female arousal. As though her desire had been hot-wired to respond only to Vidal's touch, her body moved to the rhythm he was imposing on it, the lamplight giving her naked flesh a softly golden sheen highlighted by the arousal-induced flush that bathed her chest and throat.

A voice inside Vidal's head urged him to stop, telling him that it was his duty to deny himself the pleasure that was feeding his desire for her, but that desire was too savagely primitive for him to resist. He had felt it the very first minute he had set eyes on her and seen her in the flesh—hitting him, possessing him, compelling him in a way that every fibre of his logical brain wanted to resist and deny. But now—dangerously—it had overwhelmed that logic, and he was answering to something within him that he had previously not realised existed: a male urge to conquer, to possess, to own for himself the woman he was holding and caressing. A thousand years of history and male pride, of conquest and victory, was surging through him with all the power of a burst dam, destroying every obstacle in its way.

It was that age-old instinct and drive that belonged to man's most potent needs that was compelling him now to smooth his hand over the quivering of Fliss's taut stomach and then to cup her hip as he pulled her into his own body so that her flesh could feel and know the desire it had aroused in his. On the wall, their conjoined shadows revealed the intimacy of their embrace, detailing the arch of Fliss's back as he bent her back over his arm, the aroused thrust of her nipple exposed to the lamplight, the meeting and joining of their lower bodies making them one.

Fliss was completely lost. The hard pulse of Vidal's erection felt against her bare flesh through his clothes filled her with a wanton, compulsive desire to feel his naked flesh against her own—to be able to reach out and touch him, to know him and to feel his life force.

She made no attempt to resist when Vidal picked her up and carried her over to the bed, placing her down on it. His gaze absorbed every detail of her naked body, lingering on her flesh as though he could not tear it away. A sensuality Fliss had not known she possessed caused her to move her body languidly beneath that gaze, a thrill of sweetly savage female pleasure speeding through her when she heard the stifled sound Vidal made before he joined her on the bed, holding her, shaping her, taking her mouth in an erotic kiss and keeping possession of it and her whilst he caressed her body.

The touch of his fingertips against her stomach sent jolting waves of dangerously intense delight surging through her—a delight fused with a female need to feel his touch against her even more intimately. Her body tensed, her breath locking in her lungs when Vidal's hand moved lower, covering her sex, infusing it with a heat that had her out-of-control desire for him flowering moistly in the sensitive flesh protected by the folded lips that she could feel swelling and opening beneath his hand.

Another minute—less than that, a mere handful of seconds—and he would discover her wet eagerness for his possession. And she *was* eager for it. She yearned for it, ached for it, hungered for it. In her imagination she could already feel his thrust within her, and her body was pulsing frantically under the stimulation of what she was thinking. She wanted him so much, so completely, so overwhelmingly, her desire for him was storming through her.

Vidal's own breathing was harsh and unsteady, his mouth against her skin passionately demanding. The brief grate of his teeth against her swollen nipple as he drew on it caused her body to convulse on the raw pleasure of that fierce caress. She wanted him so completely and totally that nothing else mattered.

Vidal slowly released Fliss's nipple, and then raised his head to look at her. In her eyes was all that Vidal needed to see to know that she wanted him. The look there matched the aroused anticipation of her naked body.

'Take off your clothes,' she told him huskily. 'I want to see all of you. I want to feel your skin against mine, your body against mine with nothing between us. I want you inside me, possessing me as a man should possess a woman. I want *you*, Vidal.'

Fliss listened to her own words, her own demands, with a vague sense of shock—as though they had somehow come from someone else. But Vidal didn't seem to be shocked or even surprised by them. Instead he was doing what she had asked, his gaze never leaving her face, almost pinning her to the bed as he stripped off his clothes whilst his movements allowed the light to play greedily over the stunning reality of his male flesh.

Almost wonderingly Fliss reached up to trace the line of dark body hair that bisected his torso, only stopping when he trapped her hand flat against his belly as she reached his belly button. Without a word Fliss sat up, and proceeded to retrace the path taken by her fingertips with a line of soft kisses which gradually became more intense as her own desire gripped her.

Now both her hand and her head were held immobile in Vidal's grip, their quest short-circuited, their goal denied.

Above her downbent head she could hear Vidal talking to her, his voice strained and muffled.

'I can't let you go on. Not now—not whilst my body craves the intimacy of yours so badly.'

'Yessss!' Fliss answered him fiercely. 'Yes, Vidal.'

When he released her and moved back from her, getting off the bed and reaching for the trousers he had discarded, Fliss started to reach out to him frantically, to protest—and then she stopped, her eyes widening when he removed his wallet and opened it.

It was just as well that he had taken measures to prepare himself should he have ended up in bed with Mariella, Vidal acknowledged grimly as he removed the protective sheath from its wrapper.

The interruption to their intimacy had given Fliss time to recognise what was happening— what she was doing. Away from the heat of the desire Vidal's caresses had aroused in her something about the brisk expediency of his preparations had broken the spell she had been under. The reality of what was happening was now in

stark contrast to the fantasy she had been creating. This surely was the time to stop, to be
practical and truthful and tell Vidal the truth.
But how?

She took a deep breath, and her voice was unsteady as she told him huskily, 'There's no need
for you to…to do that, because…'

Because I'm a virgin, she had intended to
continue. But before she could do so Vidal
interrupted.

'I might not be able to control the desire you
arouse in me, Felicity,' he told her harshly. 'But
I am not such a fool as to take the kind of risks
with my sexual health that intimacy with you
would involve without this protection. You may
be the sort of woman who boasts that her pleasure is increased by the danger of unprotected
intercourse, but I am not a man who wants to
put either my own or my future sexual partners'
health at risk by going down that road. Of course
if you'd prefer not to go any further…'

A horrible feeling of sickening shame was

filling her, and for a minute Fliss was tempted
to tell him to leave. But then the anger she had
felt earlier surged up inside her again, and with
it her need for justice.

Her chin lifted, and her lashes were shielding
her eyes from Vidal's scrutiny as she shrugged
and said in what she hoped was a suitably decep-
tive breathy voice. 'Not go any further now, when
you've…when I want you so much, Vidal?'

Had he been hoping that she would end it?
That she would have the strength of will that he
knew he did not? Vidal asked himself grimly,
as his body reacted immediately and openly to
her deliberate sensuality.

He could see the swollen pink softness of her
mouth, her lips half parted, and her eyes were
almost closed, as though she was already swoon-
ing with the pressure of her desire.

Anger and shame, Vidal felt them both—
against himself and against Felicity as well. But
they weren't strong enough to hold back the need
that was driving him, taking him beyond logic

and reason to a place where all that existed was his longing for this one woman.

He thrust into her slowly, needing to absorb every second of something so long denied, already knowing in that place deep within himself he had fought so hard to ignore that their bodies would match perfectly, and that hers would take and hold his in exactly the same unique way in which she already held his emotions in thrall.

He shouldn't be feeling like this. He knew what she was, after all, but it was as though something within him didn't want to recognise that reality—as though some weakness in himself refused to believe that reality and instead wanted what was happening between them to belong to them alone. His body registered and responded to what he was feeling. What he wanted… What he needed.

His earlier driven anger gave way to a longing to shed the past and take them both to a place where they could start anew, with this burning ache of mutual need and desire untouched by what had gone before. He was losing sight of what was real, Vidal warned himself. The certainty of the contempt and anger that had informed his beliefs for so long, was fracturing under the pressure of what physical intimacy with Felicity was doing to him. Deep within himself Vidal could feel the growing ache of a yearning that he couldn't banish for things to be different, for *them* to be different, so that what was happening between them could be born of...

Had he forgotten the past? Did the past really matter? Wasn't it more important that she was here now in his arms, with him in the way that he had so longed for her to be? Where was his pride? Was he really admitting to himself that he loved her?

Vidal didn't know. He only knew that holding her like this now was sweeping away the barriers he had put up against her. His pride might say that he must not love her, but what about his heart? Denial, anger, longing, loss.

Vidal felt them all—a torment of if onlys that overwhelmed him with a passionately regretful longing.

Somehow, instinctively, Fliss sensed the change within Vidal, and before she could resist it her own body was responding to it, welcoming it, wanting it, wanting *him* as the grimness of her earlier determination gave way to something far more elemental and irresistible. She wanted Vidal to feed that feeling, to caress and entice this quivering of a new and intense desire filling her. It was so much stronger than the anger-driven determination she had previously felt, Fliss thought shakily.

She was wholly unable to stop the sounds of her pleasure bubbling in her throat as her flesh responded to the building rhythmic thrust of Vidal's body within her own with increasing pleasure. That pleasure gripped her and flooded her, holding her captive, demanding her submission, making her forget why it was that their intimacy was happening.

Lost in the bitter sweetness of what might have been, Vidal tensed with disbelief when he felt the barrier within Fliss. His brain couldn't ignore the message being sent to it. In the space between one breath and the next, one thrust and the next, a confusion of thoughts exploded through his head. He looked down at Felicity, whose reactions were slower. Her flesh, softened and aching with desire, was reluctant to give up its pleasure. Resistance to the thought of being denied seized her as she realised that Vidal had stopped the delicious movement that had been giving her so much delight. In his expression she could see shock and the prospect of withdrawal. A withdrawal her body did not want.

'*No.*'

Her charged denial could have meant anything, but Fliss knew that Vidal understood it meant everything. She clung to him, urging him to complete the sensual possession he had begun, her gaze on his willing him to give her what she ached for so badly.

What was happening to her? Where was the anger she should be feeling? How had Vidal managed to steal it away from her and replace it with this aching sweetness and this longing for Vidal that now possessed her? Fliss didn't know. She wasn't capable of logical reasoned argument any more. Her feelings were too strong for that. She only knew that everything she had always wanted was here, with Vidal.

Vidal. His name and her own longing ached silently within her, her body, her flesh, clinging to his in a mute plea.

Vidal felt the quiver within Fliss that held him to her. He should end this now. There were questions that needed to be asked. Old history must be rewritten. But they were here in this moment, in this place he had wanted to take her for what felt like a lifetime. And she wanted him.

Reality had no place here. This was a place of broken dreams that could be mended, shattered hopes restored and old pain banished.

His body made its own decision, and its

possessive movement within her caused Felicity to make a soft purring sound deep in her throat. The way she was looking at him now was the way she had looked at him at sixteen, in her innocent longing. Only now her gaze was the gaze of a woman—her desire the desire of a woman. He had ached for her for so long. *Loved* her for so long. *No!* But it was too late for him to make that denial. His body wasn't listening. It was gripped by a tide it was impossible to stem.

He moved within her, carefully but surely, silencing the small sound she made as her flesh tightened in what began as pain only to be transformed into pleasure, until her body was free to respond to his possession as it wanted to. As it had been created to do, Fliss thought hectically as the world and reality began to lose focus, and there was only Vidal to cling to between waves of pleasure spiked with a need that grew with each one.

Finally the need that drove her reached its culmination in a burst of pleasure so intense that she could hardly bear it, crying out to Vidal in a tangle of words mingled with tears of release as he held her and let his own body take its pleasure in the final dying spasms of hers.

CHAPTER EIGHT

VIDAL looked into the darkness, probing it, trying to find a way through it. The bedroom was warmly lit and everything was clear. Some things were painfully clear, etched in sharp detail inside his heart for ever. The darkness he needed to probe lay within himself, within his gross negligence in not knowing. In not having known. It broke his pride, and worse than that— after all, what right did he have to pride now? Instead he was filled not just with his own pain but far more importantly with Felicity's.

The shattering of his delusion showed him how unworthy of her the love he had fought so hard against admitting actually was. Somehow he should have *known*. He would never forgive himself for that failing, and he suspected neither would Felicity.

'Am I right in thinking that the…intimacy we have just shared was at least on your part aroused by a need to punish me? To prove to me that I was wrong about you?'

'I haven't spent the last seven years plotting to be seduced by you, if that's what you mean,' Fliss parried.

They were still in bed together and, much as she would have liked to get up and protect herself by getting dressed again, she suspected that if she did Vidal would know immediately she was doing so because she felt vulnerable.

Vulnerable because her body felt almost giddily euphoric and delighted with itself, delighted with Vidal, and all too ready to explore the possibility of experiencing a repeat of the pleasure he had just given her. It was as though in place of her virginity Vidal had given her flesh a need that it believed only *he* could satisfy. And if that was true…

But, no—she must not start thinking like that. She must remember instead how she had felt before that pleasure. She must remember why it had been so important to her that Vidal confronted the reality of her virginity.

Vidal pressed her before she could say anything else. 'No more games, Felicity.' His voice was controlled and empty of emotion. 'You urged me to take your virginity not to pleasure me or even yourself but to punish me. Not as an act of intimacy, but as an act of retribution.'

Since his voice was so expressionless it was surely strange that she should feel as though he was holding within him a great weight of some hidden emotion. He was just trying to make her feel she was in the wrong, Fliss told herself. And he was doing it because he didn't want to admit that *he* was the one who had been wrong.

'You misjudged me and you kept on misjudging me,' she reminded him. 'You kept on throwing my supposed past in my face. I didn't deliberately set out to plan what happened, if that's what you think, but when the opportunity presented itself, yes—I did want it to happen.'

'You could have stopped when you recognised I had realised that you were a virgin.'

A quiver of apprehension flickered down her spine. Had he guessed that she had ended up wanting him so much that the original purpose of what she was doing had ceased to matter? That way lay fresh humiliation for her. She was twenty-three now, not sixteen, and the very idea of having secretly longed for him for all those years was not one she was prepared to entertain.

'Maybe I felt that if I did there would always be a question over the...the factual evidence, and that you might choose afterwards to believe that you had imagined my virginity.'

'Maybe?'

Fliss gave a small nervy shrug. 'What was the point in leaving things there? You've always disliked me, Vidal,' she continued before he could answer her. 'We both know that. I wanted to make sure that we both knew the truth.'

'So you remained a virgin on the off chance that the opportunity might arise for you to confront me with that truth?'

He was mocking her. Fliss was sure of it. She could feel her self-control slipping away from her.

'Have you any idea what it's like to be branded as you branded me? Not just by your words and your beliefs about me, but…but by the way in which they impacted on the way I felt about myself. I'm twenty-three. How do you think I felt about the thought of having to explain to a man I might fall in love with that I haven't had sex. He'd think I was a freak.'

'So it's my fault, is it, that you were still a virgin?'

'Yes. No. Look, I don't see the point in us discussing this. I just want to draw a line under it and move on. Like I've said, I know that you've never liked me, or the fact that I exist. You proved that when you wouldn't let me write to my father.'

'You wanted me.'

The words slipped so adroitly under her guard caused Fliss to exhale shakily in shock.

'No. I wanted justice.'

'You were aroused by me—by my touch, my possession.'

'No. I was aroused by the knowledge that you would be forced to admit you were wrong. Strong emotions can do that. After all, you don't even like me. But you…you…'

'Made love to you? Aroused you? Possessed you?'

He was too quick, his logic too sharp for her to combat right now, when all she could do was think about the delight of the pleasure he had given her. And long for a repeat of that pleasure? Desperately, Fliss struggled to find a way in which she could be as practical and unaffected by what had happened as Vidal obviously was. But the truth was that there wasn't one. The truth was that if he turned to her now and took her back in his arms…if he touched her as he had done before…

'I don't want to talk about it. I just want you to go.' No, she didn't. She wanted him to stay. She wanted him to stay and hold her and—and what? Love her? She wasn't sixteen any more, Fliss reminded herself.

Vidal closed his eyes. Why was he doing this? What was he hoping for? To force her to say she loved him in the same way that he had been forced to accept his misjudgement of her? Was that really the kind of man he was? A man whose pride demanded that she love him simply because he loved her? There was a sour taste in Vidal's mouth, a heavy weight on his heart. Hadn't he already damaged her enough?

Fliss heard Vidal exhale. Not in a sigh of regret, of course. That was impossible. She didn't trust herself to turn round and look at him when she felt him move away from her to leave the bed.

She didn't watch him either as he dressed and thankfully, finally, left the room.

Her earlier euphoria had left her now. She felt drained and empty, hollowed out emotionally apart from the forlorn ache deep inside her heart. What she wanted more than anything else was to be held in Vidal's arms, to know that what they had shared was special. Was she really so much of a fool? Was that really what she had expected? That like in some fairy story her kiss would instantly transform everything and cause Vidal to fall passionately in love with her?

Passionately in love with her? That wasn't what she wanted at all. Was it?

Wasn't there hidden away inside her the kernel of her sixteen-year-old self, with all the dreams and romantic illusions—delusions—she had then possessed? And wasn't the truth that the intimacy they had shared had left her in great danger of that kernel splitting open, so that the seed inside it could grow into new life?

Fliss buried her face in her hands, her whole

body shaking as she tried to tell herself that it was all right; she was safe and she did *not* love Vidal.

In his own room Vidal stood motionless and silent. He should really take a shower, but Felicity's scent still clung to his skin, and since that was all he would ever know of her now, apart from what was captured within his memory and his senses, he might as well indulge himself and cling to it for as long as he could. Like an adolescent overwhelmed by his first real love.

Or a man knowing his only love.

He couldn't hide from the truth any longer. He had never stopped loving Felicity.

This was the place to which his jealousy and passion had brought him. This barren place of self-loathing and regret—a true desert of the heart in which he would be for ever tormented by the mirage of what might have been. It gave him no comfort or satisfaction to know that Fliss had wanted him, or that her desire—the desire *he* had aroused in her—had ultimately overtaken whatever ideas of retribution and punishment she might claim, had kept her in his arms. He knew enough about the power of true desire to recognise it—in himself and in her. He could, had he had the stomach for it, have forced her to admit her desire for him—but what satisfaction would that have given him?

He had done her a terrible wrong in misjudging her, and there were no excuses he could plead in mitigation of that wrong, no way back to change it. He would have to live with that for the rest of his life. A second intolerable burden to add to the one he already carried, had carried for the past seven years. The burden of loving her without reason or logic and so completely that there could never ever be room in his life for another woman. There. He had admitted it now. He had loved her then and he still loved her now—had never stopped loving her, in fact, and never would.

It was the burden that Felicity herself carried,

though, that weighed most heavily on his conscience and on his heart. Out of his pride and jealousy had come the belief that by guarding her innocence until she was mature enough to receive his courtship he could eventually win the heart of the girl with whom he had fallen in love. As that young man, that arrogant and selfish man, he had not been able to bear the thought of another man taking what he had wanted and denied himself. He had been furious with Felicity for choosing another man above him, and he had misjudged and punished her for that.

CHAPTER NINE

'I SHALL leave you here to complete your examination of the house. My meeting with the water engineer should not take too long. As soon as it's finished I shall come back for you, and then we can return to Granada.'

Fliss nodded her head. Her throat felt too raw with pent-up emotion as she stood with Vidal in the hallway to her father's house. She had barely slept, and disturbingly her body, as though totally divorced from the reality of the situation between them, had reacted to his proximity in the car this morning as though they were real lovers, aching to be close to him. Several times she had felt herself being drawn to move nearer to him, her senses craving the intimacy of just being close.

Was it always like this after having sex? Was there always this need for continued closeness? This desire to touch and be touched? To be held and to know that that other person shared your thoughts and feelings? Somehow Fliss did not think so—which meant...

'This morning I couldn't find my mother's locket.' She rushed into speech in an attempt to block from her thoughts memories of their intimacy, but simply referring to the initial cause of it was enough to have her whole body burning—and not just burning but aching as well.

'I have it. The catch is faulty. I shall get it repaired for you in Granada.'

'Thank you.'

'Before I leave you, there's something I must say.'

Fliss had never seen Vidal look more grimly stern, never heard his voice contain such harshness—not even on that dreadful evening when he had looked down at her with such cruel contempt as she lay trapped in Rory's hold.

Automatically she tensed, as though waiting for a blow to fall, so Vidal's next words came as an unexpected shock.

'I owe you an apology—and an explanation. I realise that there are no words that can undo what has been done. No amount of explanation or acknowledgement of blame on my part can give you back the years you have lost when you should have been free to...to enjoy your womanhood. All I can do is hope that whatever satisfaction you took from last night is sufficient to free you from the pain I inflicted on you in the past.'

Although Fliss had flinched over that word *satisfaction*, not really sure if he was trying to subtly taunt her by referring to the sexual delight he had given her, she managed not to betray herself in any other way.

'The accusation I made against you that evening was born of my...my pride and not your behaviour. You had looked at me with an innocent desire and...'

'And because of that you thought I was pro-miscuous?' Fliss finished for him. Her face was burning over his reference to her 'innocent desire', but much as she wanted to refute it she knew that she couldn't. That was definitely not a subject she wanted him to dwell on, so she told him fiercely, 'There's no need for you to say any more. I know what motivated you, Vidal. You disliked and disapproved of me even before you met me.'

'That's not true.'

'Yes, it is. You wanted to stop me from writing to my father, remember?'

'That was—'

'That was how you felt about me. I wasn't good enough to write to my father—just as my mother hadn't been good enough to marry him. Well, at least my father had second thoughts about our relationship, even if *you* still wish it didn't exist.'

For her sake maybe it was better to allow her to believe what she was saying, Vidal decided.

It could not undo the harm that had been done, of course. Nothing could do that. But he could not and would not burden her with his love—a love she did not want. She desired him, though. Perhaps he was late in recognising that loving her meant putting her happiness first, but now that he *had* recognised that it would be shameful and wrong of him to use her first taste of adult desire as a means of trying to persuade her that she could grow to love him. He couldn't do that. Not even if it meant watching whilst she walked away from him.

The empty house, as though its silence had been disturbed by her arrival, had ultimately settled and sighed around her in the way old houses do, reminding her of the similar sighs and creaks she had experienced from her old family home when she had walked round it one last time before saying her final goodbye to it. Fliss had thought of her mother and her father as she'd walked from room to room, her sadness for them and for all that they had never had filling her emotions and her thoughts. Two gentle people who had simply not been strong enough to fight against those who had not wanted them to be together.

But she was the living proof that their love had once existed, she reminded herself as she stood in the doorway of the house's master bedroom. Not her father's bedroom. According to Vidal, her father had preferred to sleep in a smaller room, almost cell-like in its simplicity, further down the corridor. A room that in its starkness told her nothing about the man responsible for her existence.

Now, with her exploration of the house complete, she had nothing to do other than wait for Vidal to return. Nothing to do, that was, other than try not to think about the intimacy they had shared. As a sixteen-year-old she had spent many private hours in fevered imaginings of Vidal making love to her. Now that he had… Now that he had she wanted him to do it again— and again. She wanted the pleasure he had given her to be hers exclusively, wanted Vidal himself to be hers exclusively.

What had she done to herself? Fliss wondered bitterly. In proving to Vidal that he had misjudged her she had simply exchanged one emotional burden for another. Now she had no anger with which to conceal her real feelings for Vidal. Her *real* feelings? Could one fall in love for life at sixteen? Could one really know that the possession of one's first lover, was the only possession one would ever want? Her heart and her senses gave her their answer immediately and forcefully. She loved Vidal, and her anger against him for misjudging her was entangled with her pain because he did not love her back.

She loved Vidal.

From the window of the master bedroom she could see a car coming down the rutted driveway and heading for the house. Vidal's car. He had come to collect her, as he had told her he would, and soon they would be on their way back to

Granada. Soon she would be on her way back to London and her own life there. A life without Vidal. Could she bear that? She would have to.

Fliss reached the hallway just as Vidal opened the front door. His, 'Have you seen everything you wanted to see?' elicited a nod of her head.

She didn't trust herself to actually speak to him—not right now, with her heart aching for him and for his love.

Later that day, driving away from the *castillo* and the estate, Fliss knew that from now on whenever she smelled the scent of citrus fruit she would think of the Lecrin Valley, of the touch of Vidal's hands on her skin, the passion of his kiss on her mouth, and the possession of her body by his. Bittersweet pleasure, indeed.

CHAPTER TEN

THE Granada townhouse contained an air of impatient bustle—due, Fliss knew, to the fact that its lord and master was about to fly to Chile for a business meeting with his business partner there later in the week.

'It's foolish, I know, but I can't help feeling a little anxious whenever I know that Vidal is about to fly to South America. It always reminds me of the death of his father, and makes me worry for Vidal's safety—although I can never say that to Vidal himself, of course. He would think me overprotective,' the Duchess confided to Fliss as they had their morning coffee together out on the courtyard terrace, two days after Fliss's return from the *castillo*. 'You will be returning to England soon, I expect,' she added, 'but you must keep in touch with us, Fliss. You are part of the family, after all.'

Part of the family? Vidal certainly didn't want her to be part of the family.

As though her thoughts had somehow conjured him up, Vidal himself walked out of the house and came over to join them, bending swiftly to kiss his mother's cheek and smile at her. His look for Fliss was notably cold and dismissive.

'I've arranged for you to see Señor Gonzales tomorrow morning, so that the paperwork with regard to the sale of your father's house to me can be set in motion,' he told her.

'I'm not going to sell it.'

The words were out of their own volition, spoken as though Fliss had no control over them, shocking her as much as they obviously infuriated Vidal. Until that moment it had never occurred to Fliss to even *think* of keeping her father's house, but now that she had told Vidal that she wasn't going to sell it, defying what she knew were his expectations, she suddenly realised how right it felt that she should keep it.

Almost as though they had physically reached out and touched her, she felt as though somehow she could sense her parents' approval and delight. They *wanted* her to keep the house. She felt that more surely than she had ever felt anything before in the whole of her life. In a rush of aching emotion Fliss knew that no matter how much Vidal tried to bend her to his will and make her sell the house to him she wouldn't— because quite simply she couldn't.

'The dower house is part of the ducal estate,' Vidal told her grimly. 'When it was given to Felipe—'

'When my father left it to me,' Fliss interrupted him, 'he did it because he wanted me to have it. If he had wanted it returned to the estate then that's what he would have done. It's mine, and I intend to keep it.'

'To spite me?' Vidal suggested coldly.

'No,' Fliss denied. 'I intend to keep the house

for myself…for…for my children. So that they at least can know something of their Spanish ancestry.'

What children? An inner voice mocked her. The only children she wanted were Vidal's children—children she would never be allowed to have. But her words seemed to have been enough to infuriate Vidal further. Fliss could see that.

His eyes burned molten gold with anger as he challenged her, 'And these children—you will bring them here to Spain, will you? With the man who has given them to you?'

'Yes!' Fliss told him, refusing to be intimidated. 'Why shouldn't I? My father left the house to me because he wanted me to have something of him to cherish. Of course I will want to share that with my own children.' Overwhelmed by what she was feeling, she accused him emotionally, 'You might have been able to stop me making contact with my father, but you couldn't prevent him from leaving his house to me— although no doubt you tried.'

Fliss couldn't say any more. She simply couldn't trust herself to speak. Shaking her head, she got up from the table and almost ran into the house in her desperation to escape from Vidal's presence before she broke down completely.

Only when she had reached the safety and privacy of her bedroom did she let her feelings get the better of her.

And then her bedroom door opened, and she froze with disbelief as Vidal strode in.

This time he hadn't bothered knocking. This time he'd simply flung the door open and marched in, slamming the door behind him.

He was angry—furiously, savagely, passionately angry. Fliss could see it and something within her leapt to match those feelings—a wild, tempestuous intensity of emotion that had her facing him defiantly.

'I don't know what you want, Vidal—'

He didn't let her get any further. 'Don't you? Then let me show you.'

He had closed the distance between them

before she knew it, reaching for her, with a man's passion, a man's need, she recognised dizzily.

'*This* is what I want, Felicity, and you want it too. So don't even bother trying to pretend that you don't. I felt it, saw it, *tasted* it in you, and it's still there now. Didn't it ever occur to you that in giving yourself to me you might have unleashed something that neither of us can control? Something for which we will both have to pay a price? No, of course it didn't. Just as it obviously never occurred to you that a man who is aroused to possessive jealousy at the sight of the sixteen-year-old girl he wants but has denied himself, out of the moral belief that she is too young, might just leap to the wrong judgement when he finds her in bed with someone else.'

What was he doing? He shouldn't be in here, saying things like this. He should be keeping as much distance between Felicity and himself as he could. It had been those words she had thrown at him about wanting to keep her father's house for her children that had done it—the anguish of the thought of her with another man's child, conceiving that child, bearing it, loving it as she loved the man who had given it to her, had been more than he could bear. The voice within him that was urging him to stop, to leave now whilst he still could, was being drowned out by the pain of his longing for her.

'I wasn't in bed with Rory,' was the only protest Fliss could manage to make, and even that was a whispered flurry of words whilst her mind, her body, her senses grappled with exactly what Vidal had just said to her.

Vidal wanted her, desired her? Had been jealous at the thought of her with someone else?

'I promised myself I wouldn't do this,' Vidal was saying angrily. 'I told myself that it demeans me as a man to use the sexual desire we feel for one another for such a purpose. But you leave me with no other choice.'

'I leave you with no other choice?'

She wasn't going to let herself think about what he had just said—about them sharing a sexual desire for one another—and she certainly wasn't going to think about the effervescent surge of joyous delight his words had given her. Instead she would focus on the practical and the logical, on the sheer arrogance of his belief that he could walk in here and expect... What exactly *did* he expect?

Her body had started to overheat, and her thoughts were spinning out of control, wild, sensual, erotic and very dangerous thoughts that wanted to send her into his arms, into his possession.

'Not when you throw in my face your plans for the future. A future that includes taking a lover who will give you his children. He may give you that, but first I shall give you *this*, and you will give me the passion you promised all those years ago. Don't bother trying to deny it. You have already shown that you want me.'

'Any woman worth her salt can fake an org...sexual pleasure,' Fliss corrected herself frantically.

'Anyone male or female can say the words and act out a fiction of sexual delight, but the human body does not lie. And your body wanted me. It welcomed me, it ached and yearned for me, and when the moment came it showed me that I had given it pleasure. As I shall do again now. And you will not stop me, because you will not wish to stop me, even though you might try to tell yourself that you do.'

Fliss made a small mewling sound in her throat, but it was too late to protest more strongly because Vidal was kissing her, fiercely and passionately, and she was kissing him back with equal hunger and need.

Vidal's hand cupped her breast, his fingers finding her already erect nipple.

This was the last thing she had expected—and yet the first thing she had wanted. She couldn't deny it. She still tried to, though, but the words didn't come. Her body, her senses, her emotions were already saying yes.

Vidal acknowledged how hard he had tried to

fight the need for her that was sweeping over him right now, and how completely he had failed. He hadn't planned for this to happen. In fact he had done everything he could to avoid it happening. But right now he was no more able to control his need for her than she was able to conceal her response to him.

Pointless. Pointless to fight, pointless to flee, and even more pointless to allow herself to love him—and that was exactly what she was doing, Fliss recognised, as Vidal looked deep into her eyes and then kissed her slowly and lingeringly. The sensation of his mouth moving on hers with such deliberate and controlled sensuality was stealing her resistance from her. All she wanted to do was respond to him, give to him, be held and touched and possessed by him. The force of that need made her whole body tremble in his arms like a reed in the wind, needing his support to protect her from her own vulnerability.

Vidal moved back and pulled off his shirt, then cupped her face and kissed the side of her neck, sending hot shivers of pleasure running over her skin so that her control ran from her like sand taken by a ceaseless and unstoppable tide.

'Touch me,' he whispered against her ear, and that rough, broken note of urgency suggested that his whole desire was for her touch and he was on the point of breaking his self-control. Surely more a figment of her own imagination than true reality? But Vidal was lifting her hand and placing it against the warm flesh of his chest, holding it there as he implored her, 'Touch me, Fliss, as I've wanted you to touch me from the moment I saw you.'

Unable to stop herself, Fliss obeyed his whispered command. Wasn't this, after all, what she had ached and longed for herself? Now, as she stroked and explored her way over Vidal's torso, she could feel the surge of the blood beneath his skin rising up to meet the trembling excitement of her fingertips—just as she could feel the movement of his muscles as she grew bolder and explored further and lower, to the flat plane where his flesh disappeared beneath the edge of his chinos.

'Yes.' The heated urgency of the demand Vidal smothered against the rise of her breast came just when her hand reached the barrier of his trousers, and could only mean one thing. But still Fliss hesitated. To have come this far was dangerous. To go any further would be fatal, taking her to a state of being and emotion that once inhabited she knew she would never want to leave.

'So you still want to torment me, do you?' Vidal accused her. 'Then maybe I should do a little tormenting of my own.'

Before she could stop him he had swung her up into his arms and was carrying her into his own bedroom, minimalist and masculine in design and decor, even if the large bed on which he was placing her seemed to Fliss to be the most sensually dangerous place she had ever known. Or was that because Vidal was now undressing her and himself, between kisses she was sure were designed to arouse her to the point where she ached for him so much that she was willing to do anything to have the pleasure he was giving her? Each kiss, each touch was taking her deeper and deeper into a place of such intense need that nothing else existed, and her now naked body was trembling with the force of her longing.

'See how much you want me?' Vidal asked her.

Fliss couldn't deny it. She did want him. She wanted him, needed him, longed for him, loved him.

Her body shuddered in mute confirmation of that admission.

Vidal leaned forward and stroked her body from her hip to her breast with a fiercely de-manding caress that ended with him bending his head to take her nipple between his lips, drawing the need up through her body until it was trembling and pulsing in response to him. His free hand was cupping her other breast, his knee urging her legs apart.

The desire that ripped into her was a volcano of molten heat. The satisfaction of feeling his naked erect flesh against her own sex, initially so pleasurable, quickly became another form of exquisite torture as she ached for even more intimacy, grinding her lower body against him whilst Vidal in turn lifted her against himself, opening her legs to wrap them around his body and hold him closer.

Fliss craved the sensation of him within her, the movement of his flesh inside and against her own. Just the thought of it made need surge through her in unbearable longing, but Vidal was pushing her away, removing himself from her, leaving her. Was this what he had meant about tormenting her?

Yearningly Fliss reached to him, but he shook his head.

'Not yet,' he told her softly. 'I want to touch all of you, to taste all of you, to know all of you first.'

He was stringing kisses along the back of her

knee and then the inside of her leg, whilst his fingers stroked apart the willing swollen heat of the lips covering her sex. The pulse already beating there increased in intensity, driving her towards the goal her body now craved. The caress of Vidal's touch against the intimate wetness of her sex was both a pleasure and an incitement to want more, to want *him*. Fliss knew it as she curled her fingers round his wrist in a mute plea for what she really wanted.

Vidal denied her, bending his head and dipping his tongue into the moist arousal of her sex, lightly caressing the very heart of it, and then less lightly, whilst Fliss clung to what was left of her reason until she could cling to it no more, and then her cries for him to complete the pleasure he was giving her with the stroke of his flesh within her rose and fell against the fevered backdrop of their unsteady breathing and the inward clamour of their frantic heartbeats.

'Now! *Now*,' Fliss begged Vidal, all control and restraint lost as she was sucked into the maelstrom of desire Vidal had aroused within her. Her senses, already stimulated and aroused, absorbed the reality of his maleness as he stopped, poised over her, wantonly glorying in awareness of his need, of his erection taut and hard.

Fliss shivered in an agony of pleasure as she felt the strength of it pressing against the entrance to her own body. Her sex ached with longing, its muscles quivering in eager anticipation of the pleasure his possession of her promised. His first swift, urgent thrust made her cry out in a paroxysm of heart-stopping pleasure. Her body waited on the crest of that pleasure for more of what it craved.

Another thrust—deeper, harder—had her body tightening around him.

Her fiercely passionate 'yes' was breathed against Vidal's mouth, her longing and arousal overwhelming her completely.

'You want me,' he told her.

'Yes. Yes. I want you now, Vidal. I need you

now.' The hot, passionate words tumbled from her lips as she clung to him, holding him within her, trembling with pleasure and anticipation.

'Tell me again,' he urged as he stroked deeper inside her. 'Tell me how much you want me.'

'So much—too much. More than there are words for,' Fliss told him as she pressed frantic kisses against his face.

Now he was moving within her, satisfying her need and yet increasing it at the same time. Helplessly Fliss clung to him as the tension within her grew, until it possessed every bit of her, every pulse of her blood and her heart, all that she was. And then all at once it was there, a brief second of hanging in space, and then the implosion, the fierce contraction of her body that took her over the edge of arousal and into the eye of a storm. Her orgasm was shot through with the pulse of Vidal's release.

Lost in the wonder of their closeness, helpless and vulnerable to all that she was feeling, Fliss clung to Vidal, knowing that this wasn't desire alone that possessed her, this was *love*. And his feelings for her?

Against her ear she could feel the warmth of his breath. Her voice trembled as she whispered softly, 'Vidal?'

Vidal's chest tightened. He could hear the emotion in Felicity's voice. The way it had trembled when she had said his name had felt like a physical caress against his skin. That emotion, though, came from the satisfaction of desire. Nothing else.

He exhaled slowly. Taking another deep breath, he told her curtly, 'Now we are even. You used my desire for you to prove that I misjudged you. Now I have used yours for me to prove that you lied when you said you didn't want me.'

Fliss could hear Vidal speaking coldly as she lay there, still wrapped in the vulnerability of loving him so intimately and intensely, wholly unable to protect herself from the cruelty of what he was saying now.

CHAPTER ELEVEN

SHE couldn't lie here like this for ever, in the grip of a grief so intense that it went way beyond the release of any tears, Fliss told herself. She must have showered and dressed after Vidal had gone, she recognised, but she had no memory of having done so. All she could remember was his final words to her, his final cruelty. She had been crazy to think that what had happened between them just now could change anything. He hated her.

Someone was knocking on the bedroom door. Fliss stiffened, and then trembled. Had Vidal come back? Did he want to utter more cruel words? Her heart pounded with pain. There was a second knock on the door. She would have to answer it. She got to her feet and walked unsteadily towards the door, exhaling with what she told herself was relief when she opened it to find the Duchess standing outside in the corridor, her face creased with tension.

'Can I come in?' the Duchess asked. 'Only there's something I have to say to you—about Vidal and what you said earlier.'

Numbly Fliss realised that in the heat of the moment, when she had been arguing with Vidal earlier, she had completely forgotten that his mother was also there—a silent witness to the accusations Fliss had made against her son. Unable to do anything else, she nodded her head and held open the door, closing it once the Duchess was in the room.

'I had to speak to you,' the Duchess told Fliss as she sat in one of the chairs by the fire, obliging Fliss to take the other or be left standing over her visitor. 'No mother likes to hear her child being spoken of as you spoke of Vidal earlier. You will learn that for yourself one day. But it is not just for Vidal's sake that I want to talk to you, Felicity. It is for your own as well. Bitterness and resentment are destructive. They can eat away at a person until there is nothing left but those destructive emotions. I would hate to think of such damaging emotions destroying you—especially when those feelings are not necessary.'

'I'm sorry if I hurt or offended you,' Fliss apologised. 'That wasn't my intention. But the way Vidal has behaved—preventing me from making contact with my father—'

'No, that is not true. It was not Vidal. On the contrary, in fact. You owe Vidal so much, and it is thanks to him that you have had— Oh!'

Guiltily the Duchess placed her hand over her mouth, shaking her head.

'I only came up here to defend Vidal, not to… But I've let my emotions run away with me. Please forget what I said.'

Forget? How could she. '*What* is not true?' Fliss demanded, urgently. 'And what do I owe him? Please, tell me.'

'I can't say any more,' the Duchess answered, very obviously flustered and uncomfortable. 'I have said too much already.'

'You can't say something like that and then not explain,' Fliss protested, feeling equally emotional.

'I'm sorry,' the Duchess apologised. 'I shouldn't have come up here. Oh, I am so cross with myself. I'm sorry, Fliss. I really am.' She got up and walked towards the door, pausing there before opening it to repeat softly, 'I really am sorry.'

Fliss stared at the closed door. What had the Duchess meant? What was it she had started to say and then refused to tell her? It was, of course, only natural that a mother should defend her child, Fliss could understand that. But there had been much more than maternal protection in the Duchess's voice. There had been certainty, knowledge. A knowledge that *she* did not have. What kind of knowledge? Something to do with Fliss's father? Something to do with the fact that Fliss had never been allowed to contact him?

Something she had a right to know. Something that only one person could tell her, if she had the courage to demand an answer.

Vidal himself. And *did* she have that courage?

The Duchess's slip made Fliss feel as though a secret door had suddenly appeared in a room she had thought she knew so well that it could not hide any secrets. It was an unnerving, uncomfortable experience. There was probably nothing for her to discover, no secrets for her to learn, no darkness for her to fear beyond that secret door. But what if there was? What if…? What *could* there be? Vidal had told her himself that he had intercepted her letter to her father and that she was not to write to him again. The evidence had spoken for itself. Hadn't it?

She needed to talk to Vidal, Fliss recognised.

Vidal was in his own suite of rooms, working, Rosa informed Fliss in a tone that suggested he would not want to be interrupted, when Fliss asked her where he was.

Not giving herself time to change her mind, Fliss started to climb the stairs. All the way up her stomach was cramping and her knees were almost knocking. Her mouth was dry with apprehension.

As she walked along the corridor, part of her wanted her to turn round, her courage almost failing her. The door to Vidal's rooms was slightly ajar. Fliss knocked on it hesitantly and then waited, a cowardly relief filling her when there was no immediate reply.

Letting her hand fall to her side, she was just about to step back from the door when she heard Vidal call out briskly in Spanish from inside the room, in a voice that commanded obedience, for her to enter.

Feeling decidedly unsteady, Fliss turned the handle.

She might not have touched any alcohol, but

she felt slightly light-headed—light-headed and, she recognised, rather dangerously emotional.

The first thing she realised as she stepped into the room and let the door swing shut behind her was that this room was decorated in a far more modern and pared-down fashion than the rest of the house, in shades of grey and off-white, and was furnished as a functional working office. The second was that Vidal was standing in the doorway between the room she was in and a shower room adjacent to it, with only a towel wrapped round his damp body, and he was looking at her in a way that told her that her presence was neither expected nor wanted.

Unable to say anything, but helpless with longing and love, and humiliatingly aware that she was in danger of betraying everything that he made her feel, Fliss forced herself to drag her gaze away.

Only now did it dawn on her that Vidal had instructed her to come in in Spanish because he had assumed she was one of the servants. He certainly wasn't at all pleased to see her. She could tell that from the grim expression on his face.

To her dismay he was actually turning away from her, about to walk off.

'No!' Fliss protested, darting forward and then coming to an abrupt halt when he turned round so quickly that only a couple of feet separated them. 'I want to talk to you. There's something I want to know.'

'Which is?

Why did you stop me communicating with my father? That was what Fliss had intended to ask him but for some reason she heard herself saying instead, 'Was it really you who stopped me from making contact with my father?'

The silence in the room was electric, the air almost humming with Vidal's tension, and Fliss knew immediately from his unmoving silence that her question had caught him off-guard.

'What makes you ask me that?'

Should she lie to him and say it was just

curiosity? If she wanted to hear the truth from him then maybe she should start the ball rolling by offering him her own truth first. Fliss took a deep breath. 'Something your mother let slip, by accident, that made me think what I've always assumed to be fact might not be.'

'When the decision was taken it was done with your best interests in mind,' Vidal told her obliquely.

He was choosing his words carefully—too carefully, Fliss realised. Too carefully and in a way that suggested to her that he was concealing something—or protecting someone?

'Who took that decision?' she demanded, adding fiercely, 'I have a right to know, Vidal. I have a right to know who made that decision and why it was made. If you don't tell me I will go back and ask your mother and I shall keep on asking her until she tells me,' she threatened wildly.

'You will do no such thing.'

'Then *tell* me. Was it your grandmother? My

father? It has to be one of them. There wasn't anyone else. The only other person involved was my mother…' Fliss had almost been speaking to herself, but the sudden movement of Vidal's head, the brief tensing of his jaw when she mentioned her mother, gave him away, made her stiffen and stare at him in disbelief. Her voice was a raw, emotional whisper as she demanded, 'My mother? It was my *mother*? Tell me the truth, Vidal. I want to know the truth.'

'She believed she was doing the right thing for you,' Vidal told her, sidestepping her question.

'My *mother*! But you were the one who brought my letter back. You…' Fliss felt so weak with shock and disillusionment that she couldn't help saying tremulously, 'I don't understand.'

The admission was a small agonised whisper that made Vidal want to go to her and hold her protectively, but he fought the urge. He had sworn to himself that he must allow her to have her freedom, that he must not impose on her the burden of his love for her. It was hard, though, to see her so distressed and not be able to offer her the comfort he longed to give her.

Instead all he could do was say quietly, 'Let me try to explain.'

Fliss nodded her head, sinking down into the nearest chair. Her thoughts and her emotions were in total disarray, and yet totally focused on what her questions had revealed. But still there was something about the sight of Vidal wearing only that towel around his hips that touched her senses as though they were a raw wound, reminding her of all that she could never have.

'After my father's death, control of the family's affairs and finances passed back to my grandmother. I was a minor, and my grandmother was my trustee along with the family solicitor. My grandmother's treatment of your father, combined with her refusal to help your mother financially or recognise you, resulted in your father having what was in effect a minor breakdown. Your father was a kind, loving man, Felicity, but sadly his mental health was damaged by my grandmother's determination to ensure he married well. He was a very gifted amateur historian, and as a young man he wanted to pursue a career in that field. My grandmother refused. She told him that it wasn't acceptable for him to take up any kind of paid occupation. As I said before, your father was a kind and gentle man, but my grandmother was a strong-willed woman who rode roughshod over everyone and thought she was doing the right thing. She bullied and cowed him from the moment she realised he wanted to choose his own path in life. She never allowed him to forget that she was trying to do what his birth mother would have wanted for him, and that caused so much guilt and confusion in him. That was why he gave up your mother so easily, and I believe it was also why he had a breakdown when he learned of your mother's pregnancy. He wanted to be with you both so much, but he could not stand up to my grandmother. He never recovered fully from that breakdown.'

Fliss could hear the sadness and the regret in Vidal's voice and recognised that he had cared a great deal about her father.

'I have never ceased to feel guilty that it was my thoughtless comment that provoked my grandmother into questioning Felipe and your mother about their relationship. And I never will.'

That Vidal should make such an admission caused Fliss's heart to ache for the pain she could tell he felt.

'You were a child,' she reminded him. 'My mother told me that she felt your grandmother had her own suspicions about her and my father anyway.'

'Yes, she told me the same thing when I first visited her—after my grandmother's death. Her kindness was balm to my guilt.'

'When you first visited her?' Fliss questioned. 'When was that?'

She could see from Vidal's frown that he had said more than he'd intended. His voice was clipped, his words sparing, as though he was being forced to say more than he wished to say, when he told her, almost reluctantly, 'After my grandmother's death I visited your mother. As head of the family it was my duty to…to do so—to ensure that both you and she—'

'You came to England to see my mother?' Fliss interrupted him.

'Yes. I thought she might want to have news of your father. The manner in which they had been parted had not been…kind, and there was you to consider—their child. I wanted your mother to know that you and she would be made very welcome if she were to choose to bring you to Spain. I thought she might want your father to see you, and you to meet him.'

Vidal was trying to choose his words very carefully. Felicity had suffered so much pain already. He didn't want to inflict still more on her.

Fliss, though, had guessed what Vidal was trying to shield her from.

'My mother didn't want to go back to Spain? She didn't want me to meet my father?' she guessed.

Vidal immediately defended Fliss's mother. ''She was thinking of you. I'd had to tell her about Felipe's breakdown, and she was concerned about the effect that might have on you.'

'There's more, isn't there? I want to know it all,' Fliss insisted.

For a minute she thought that Vidal would refuse. He turned away from her to look towards the window.

'I have a right to know.' Fliss persisted.

She heard Vidal sigh.

'Very well, then. But remember, Felicity, all your mother wanted to do was protect you.'

'Nothing you can tell me will change how I feel about my mother,' Fliss assured him truthfully. And nothing could change how she felt about Vidal either, she knew. He had misjudged her, and it seemed she had misjudged him, but her love for him remained as true now as it had been all those years ago.

Vidal turned back to look at her. Fliss held her breath. Could he somehow read in her eyes her love for him? Quickly she dropped her lashes to conceal her expression.

'Your mother told me that she did not want there to be any contact between you and the Spanish side of your family,' Vidal began. 'She asked me to give her my promise that there would not be. Initially she was afraid that it might lead to you being hurt. You were a young girl, with perhaps an idealised vision of your father that she recognised he could not match, and then later she was equally afraid that you might—out of daughterly love—sacrifice your own freedom to be with your father. I gave her the promise she asked for, so when your letter to your father arrived—'

'You kept it from my father. Yes, I can understand that now, Vidal. But why didn't you simply destroy it? Why did you bring it to England and...and taunt me with it?'

The pain in her voice cut into Vidal's heart.

'I thought it best to discuss the situation with your mother in person. I didn't intend to *taunt* you, as you put it, I merely wanted to ensure that you did not write to your father again.'

'You came all the way to England just to discuss that?'

Vidal made a small dismissive gesture with one hand, as though to sweep her question away, and immediately Fliss knew.

'You didn't just come for that, did you? There was something else.'

There was another pause whilst Vidal once again looked towards the window before turning back to tell her, 'As I said earlier, as head of the family I felt it my duty. Your mother had had a very difficult time, enduring the loss of the man she loved, and the totally unacceptable financial hardship she had to suffer before...'

'Before she inherited all that money,' Fliss

said slowly. 'Money from an aunt who Mum had never once mentioned to me and who I never met. Money that Mum often said she was grateful to have because of all that it would do for me. Money to buy us a lovely house in the country that she said was especially for me. Money that meant Mum didn't have to work so that she could be there for me. Money to send me to a good school and then university.'

Her mind was frantically scrambling over small facts and clues that suddenly, when put together, created a potential truth that shocked her to the core.

'There was no wealthy aunt, was there?' she challenged Vidal in a small bleak voice. 'There was no aunt, no will, no inheritance. It was *you*. You paid for everything...'

'Felicity—'

'It's true, isn't it?' Fliss demanded. The blood had drained from her face, leaving shadows beneath the curve of her cheekbones. 'It's true,' she repeated insistently. 'You were the one who bought the house, who gave Mum an allowance, who paid for my education.'

'You and your mother had every right to what I provided for you. I was only redressing the wrong done to you by my grandmother. Your mother was reluctant to accept anything from me at first, but I told her then as I tell you now that it would only have added to the guilt the family was already carrying if you were not given something of what should have been yours.'

'I've been so wrong about you.' Fliss's throat was so raw with emotion she could hardly speak. 'I've misjudged you so badly.'

She was so agitated that she stood up to pace the small area in front of the chair, almost wringing her hands in her despair.

'No, Fliss. You simply misinterpreted the facts as you saw them. That is all. I am the one who has been guilty of misjudgement—and a far greater misjudgement than yours.'

'Please don't be kind to me,' Fliss begged. 'It just makes things worse.'

How much worse only she could be allowed to know. Now she could see Vidal as he really was, instead of coloured by her own erroneous beliefs. Now she could see how tall he stood, how honourable he was, and how truly empty her life would be without him in it.

'I want you to have my father's house,' she told Vidal. 'I don't want any money for it. It's right that it should return to being part of the estate. I'm going home, Vidal.' she added. 'As soon as it can be arranged.'

'Felicity—'

Vidal took a step towards her, causing Fliss to step back. If he touched her now she would fall apart. She just knew it.

'I can't stay here now.'

'You've had a shock. It isn't wise to make decisions in the heat of the moment.'

As he spoke Vidal was reaching out to her. Another second and he would be touching her. She couldn't let that happen. She didn't dare.

Fliss stepped back, forgetting that the chair

was there, and would have fallen over it if Vidal hadn't grabbed hold of her.

She could hear the heavy thud of his heartbeat, smell the warm scent of his skin. He was only holding her arms, but the whole of her body was responding to being so close to him, yearning and aching for him.

Fliss moved to pull back from him, and then gasped when instead of releasing her Vidal's hold on her tightened. She looked up at him, her eyes widening as he lowered his head towards her. His breath seared her lips. Sensual heat flooded her body.

'No,' Fliss protested, but her protest was lost beneath the passion of his kiss.

She wanted Vidal so much. She loved him so much. But Vidal did not love her.

'No!' Fliss cried out, pushing him away. 'Don't touch me. I can't bear it. I've got to leave, Vidal, I love you too much to stay—'

Horrified by what she had revealed, Fliss could

only stare up at Vidal, who was standing as still as a statue, looking back at her.

'What did you say?' Vidal's voice was harsh.

He was angry with her, and no wonder, Fliss thought. She had embarrassed him and made a fool of herself.

'What did you say?' Vidal repeated.

In a panic, Fliss stepped back from him, shaking her head as she fibbed, 'I didn't say anything.'

Vidal had stepped back from her, but now he was closing the distance between them.

'Yes, you did.' His topaz gaze held hers. 'You said you loved me.'

Fliss had had enough. Her self-control was at breaking point and her heart felt as though it was already broken. What did her pride matter now, when she had already lost so much?

Lifting her head, she told Vidal, 'All right, yes, I *do* love you. The children I want to have—the children I want to know their Spanish heritage—are your children, Vidal. Don't blame me if you don't want to know any of this, if you don't want to hear. You made me tell you.'

'Not want to know? Not want to hear the words I've been aching to hear since you were sixteen years old?'

'What?' Now it was Fliss's turn to question him. 'You don't mean that,' she protested.

'I mean it more than I've ever meant anything in my life.' Vidal assured her. 'The truth is that I fell in love with you when you were sixteen, but of course you were too young for a man's love, and it would have been dishonourable and very wrong of me to have spoken to you of my feelings then. I told myself that I'd wait until you were older, until you were mature enough for me to court you properly as a woman.'

'Oh, Vidal,' Fliss breathed.

'It's true,' he assured her. 'That was why I misjudged you. Because I was jealous. Jealous that someone else had taken you from me. I did you a terrible wrong, Fliss. I don't deserve your love.'

Fliss could see that he meant what he was saying, and her heart ached for him.

'Yes, you do,' she insisted. 'And if I'd known then how you really felt about me, I suspect I'd have done everything I could to persuade you to change your mind.'

'That is what I was afraid of,' Vidal admitted tenderly. 'It would have been the wrong thing to do for both of us but especially for you.'

When Fliss started to protest, Vidal stopped her.

'You were too young. It would have been wrong. But hearing that boy boasting in the way that he did sent me a little mad, I think. I told myself afterwards that the girl I loved didn't exist, that I'd created her inside my own imagination. I told myself I should be glad that you were not the innocent I had thought, because had you been my self-control might have betrayed me and I might, out of my love for you, have broken the trust your mother had in me.'

'So you stopped loving me?'

'I tried to tell myself I had, but the reality is that I ached and longed for you. Only my pride kept me away from you—especially when your mother died. You haunted my dreams and made it impossible for me to put any other woman in your place. I resigned myself to living without love, and then you walked back into my life. I knew that everything my pride had told me about the impossibility of loving you was a lie. I loved you no matter what. I realised that that first time we were in bed together—before I realised that I had misjudged you. I wanted to tell you how much I loved you, but I felt it would be wrong to burden you with my love. I wanted you to have the freedom to make your own choices, free of any burdens from the past.'

'You are my choice, Vidal. You are my love, and you always will be.'

'Are you really sure that I am what you want?' Vidal asked her with unfamiliar humility.

'Yes,' Fliss told him emotionally.

'I am your first lover.'

'The only lover I want,' she said fiercely. 'The only lover I have ever wanted or will ever want.' Fliss knew as she spoke that it was true.

'I hope you mean that,' Vidal told her thickly, 'because I am not generous enough to give you a second opportunity to walk away from me.' When he saw the way Fliss was looking at him Vidal warned her in a voice rough with passion, 'Don't look at me like that.'

'Why not?' Fliss asked him mock innocently.

'Because if you do then I shall have to do this,' Vidal told her, kissing her so passionately that Fliss felt as though the desire he was arousing within her was melting her body right down to her bones.

'We've both fought so hard not to love one another, but it was obviously a fight we were destined to lose,' she told him breathlessly, once he had stopped kissing her.

'And one in which losing I know I have won

something far more precious—you, my darling,' Vidal responded, before kissing her again.

What a joy it was to know that she could respond to him with all her heart and all her love, knowing that he had given her his, Fliss thought as he kept on kissing her while he carried her over to the bed.

'I love you,' Vidal told her as he placed her on it. 'I love you and I will always love you. This is where our love begins, Felicity. Our love and our future together—if that is what you want?'

Wrapping her arms around him, Fliss whispered against his lips, 'You are what I want, Vidal, and you always will be.'

'I want you to marry me,' Vidal told her. 'Soon—as soon as it can be arranged.'

'Yes,' Fliss agreed. 'As soon as it can be arranged. But right now I want you to make love to me, Vidal.'

'Like this, do you mean?' he asked softly, as he started to undress her.

'Yes,' Fliss sighed happily. 'Exactly like that '

EPILOGUE

'HAPPY?'

Fliss raised her hand to touch Vidal's face, the wedding ring he had placed on her finger less than twenty-four hours earlier gleaming in the sunlight. Her sparkling eyes and the emotion that lit up her face gave Vidal his answer without the need for any words, but she still spoke, telling him emotionally, 'More happy that I ever believed possible.'

'Happier even than you dreamed of being at sixteen?' he teased her gently.

Fliss laughed. 'At sixteen I didn't dare dream of being married to you, Vidal.'

In several hours' time they would be boarding the private jet that would be taking them to the private tropical island where they were going to honeymoon, but right now the two of them were making a special pilgrimage, retracing together the steps taken all those years ago by her mother and her father, accompanied by young Vidal.

From the Alhambra they had strolled to the Generalife, the famous summer palace with its much-photographed water garden and its long canal and fountains bordered by beautifully tended flowerbeds. Sunlight danced on the jets of water thrown up by the fountains, and when Vidal stopped walking alongside one of them Fliss looked at him expectantly with love in her eyes.

'It was here that I saw your father take your mother's hand,' he told her softly, reaching out to take hold of Fliss's hand.

As she looked into the heart of the fountain it was almost possible for Fliss to imagine that she could see the shadowy images of those two young people.

'Our love will be deeper and stronger for knowing their story,' Vidal promised. 'Our happiness together is what they would both have wanted for us.'

'Yes,' Fliss agreed.

It might normally be forbidden, but Vidal had magically made it possible for officialdom to turn a blind eye so that there was no one to object when, very gently and carefully, Fliss opened her closed palm to allow the petals from some of the white roses from her wedding bouquet to fall into the water, where they floated gently.

'A release of the past and a welcome to the future,' Fliss told Vidal.

'*Our* future,' he responded, taking her into his arms. 'The only future I could ever want.'

MILLS & BOON PUBLISH EIGHT LARGE PRINT TITLES A MONTH. THESE ARE THE TITLES FOR JULY 2011.

A STORMY SPANISH SUMMER
Penny Jordan

TAMING THE LAST ST CLAIRE
Carole Mortimer

NOT A MARRYING MAN
Miranda Lee

THE FAR SIDE OF PARADISE
Robyn Donald

THE BABY SWAP MIRACLE
Caroline Anderson

EXPECTING ROYAL TWINS!
Melissa McClone

TO DANCE WITH A PRINCE
Cara Colter

MOLLY COOPER'S DREAM DATE
Barbara Hannay

0711 Rom LP

MILLS & BOON PUBLISH EIGHT LARGE PRINT TITLES A MONTH. THESE ARE THE TITLES FOR AUGUST 2011.

☙

JESS'S PROMISE
Lynne Graham

NOT FOR SALE
Sandra Marton

AFTER THEIR VOWS
Michelle Reid

A SPANISH AWAKENING
Kim Lawrence

IN THE AUSTRALIAN BILLIONAIRE'S ARMS
Margaret Way

ABBY AND THE BACHELOR COP
Marion Lennox

MISTY AND THE SINGLE DAD
Marion Lennox

DAYCARE MUM TO WIFE
Jennie Adams

MILLS & BOON PUBLISH EIGHT LARGE PRINT TITLES A MONTH. THESE ARE THE TITLES FOR AUGUST 2011.

JESS'S PROMISE
Lynne Graham

NOT FOR SALE
Sandra Marton

AFTER THEIR VOWS
Michelle Reid

A SPANISH AWAKENING
Kim Lawrence

IN THE AUSTRALIAN BILLIONAIRE'S ARMS
Margaret Way

ABBY AND THE BACHELOR COP
Marion Lennox

MISTY AND THE SINGLE DAD
Marion Lennox

DAYCARE MUM TO WIFE
Jennie Adams